Review Comments for
Kim Chinquee's

Shot Girls

"Kim Chinquee writes tenderly about tough women—soldiers, cops, survivors of violence—and brings a fierce empathy and lyricism to these stories of hardscrabble lives. *Shot Girls* is a remarkable collection; Chinquee is an important and necessary writer for these times." —Dan Chaon, author of *Ill Will* and *Stay Awake*

"Kim Chinquee is an American original. In *Shot Girls*, she adds to her already sterling body of work, using spare but sublime prose to tell gripping stories that reveal much about life, love and our common humanity." —Ben Bradlee, Jr, author of *The Kid: the Immortal Life of Ted Williams* and *The Forgotten: How the Abandoned People of One Pennsylvania County Elected Donald Trump and Changed America.*

"The girls and women breathing through Chinquee's pages grapple with the casual cruelty of lovers, parents, and a soul-shattering culture. Hands may be calloused and hearts broken, but pervading every bracing, beautifully crafted sentence is a quiet, insistent strength. These are women you know (maybe yourself) and *Shot Girls* is an unsentimental declaration: Here I am. See me." —Dawn Raffel, author of *The Secret Life of Objects* and *Carrying the Body*

"Kim Chinquee is a master storyteller. She brilliantly balances short-shorts and longer works. *Shot Girls* is a sensory delight." —Brandon Hobson, author of *Where The Dead Sit Talking*

"Beautifully honed stories about lives on the verge of free fall. *Shot Girls* is merciless in its frank depiction of the way our messy lives careen off one another, bruising everyone they touch. These are the stories that Raymond Carver might have written if he'd grown up female, was from the midwest, joined the military, and lived into the 21st century." —Brian Evenson, *A Collapse of Horses* and *What We Talk About When We Talk About Love: Bookmarked*

"Kim Chinquee's *Shot Girls* flings you into the jittery lives of women and menacing men, of women on the brink of disaster or anomic drift, the stink of smoke and drink, of bad or so-so sex wafting all around. Alternating between lapidary flashes and short fictions that read like novels, *Shot Girls* is a sledgehammer strike against patriarchy. Chinquee's deftly drawn dreamers and schemers, drifters and grifters, and gone nuclear families are living, loving, and lying in American pre-fab, its sordid bars and motels, empty parking lots, imposing offices, cold hospitals, and strangling military strongholds. Keenly observed and deeply affecting, *Shot Girls* is a marvelous haunting, its author a master of loneliness, beauty, desire, sadness, loss." —John Madera, *The Big Other*

"These bold stories delve into farm work, bloodwork, bar life, military service, sex, love, the possibility of men and the agility of women. Chinquee's wit and speed and clarity are thrilling." —Pia Ehrhardt, author of *Famous Fathers & Other Stories*

"Tiny stories written like jewels, long stories with endings that snap into place." —Terese Svoboda, author of *Anything That Burns You* and *Bohemian Girl*

"Stories full of danger and electric writing. Searing. Brilliant." —Susan Henderson, author of *Up From The Blue* and *The Flicker of Old Dreams*

SHOT GIRLS
by Kim Chinquee

a collection of short fiction

Also by Kim Chinquee

Oh Baby
Pistol
Pretty
Veer

Stories from this collection have been published in *War, Literature and the Arts; Ploughshares; Story Quarterly; North Dakota Quarterly; Fiction; Mississippi Review; NOON; Indiana Review; Midway Journal; Booth; Cottonwood; New World Writing; Center; New York Tyrant; Wisconsin Academy Review; The Black Mountain Review; Coffin Bell; Noo; Stone Canoe; The Pushcart Prize XXXI, Best of the Small Presses*, 2007; *The Female Complaint; The Lineup: 20 Provocative Women Writers.*

Cover design: Pier Rodelon

ISBN: 978-1-7326416-1-7
LCCN: 2018953491

First Edition

Published by Ravenna Press
ravennapress.com

To my fellow veterans. To all who serve.

Shot Girls

Contents

SERVICE

The Air Force was strange for a woman, even for me, and I'd been in eight years. I'd just moved to England with my son, Ian, to a tiny base that was supposed to do clean up after the Gulf War, only there wasn't any cleanup to do, and now they kept the place running with a skeleton staff. I was part of that. I moved to get away from my husband, Scotty, who I was trying to make my ex-husband, though he wasn't too sharp at signing the papers. My dad said maybe if I went overseas Scotty would know I was for real.

The housing was military. What that meant in England was a one-story brick duplex, the same one the Air Force builds in Biloxi, or Saudi Arabia, or Singapore. My neighbor was a career guy named Keith and he came over to see me a lot. He had two kids of his own and his wife already signed his papers. When he came over Saturday I was getting Ian ready for bed.

"How you doing?" Keith said, peeking around the corner into my doorway. "Going to bed? I mean—Ian?"

I said, "Come on in."

Keith's hair was dusty red, greenish eyes, and freckles roamed across his face. My son, Ian, waddled up as Keith stepped in.

Keith offered a high-five, and Ian looked at him, then planted his bottle back in his mouth.

Ian was almost two, too old to have a bottle, maybe, but I thought maybe it was better to let him keep it, I didn't know, so he wouldn't wonder where his father was. Then I thought maybe it was me wondering, not him.

"I wonder if he's OK," I said, following Ian into the living room.

"He looks pretty happy," Keith said. He plopped on my sofa, picked up a *Runner's World*, sifted through the pages, then flipped the TV to the USAFE station.

Ian put his hands up on the screen. He seemed amused by the crackling sound on the glass. When I pulled him back he started crying, I picked him up and said, "Shh." I rocked him a bit, which seemed to soothe him. I headed for the stairs.

"You want to hang around?" I said to Keith. "I'll be right down."

Ian kicked, clutching his bottle.

Upstairs I stopped in the hall bath and checked myself in the mirror. I looked a little bedraggled.

"Sweetheart," I said to Ian, "it's time for bed." I straightened my hair with my fingers.

I put Ian in his crib and twisted the knob of the music box that Scotty's mother had given us. Ian stood in his crib, grabbed the rails, yelling out my name—he never called me Mommy, but Beth, because other people called me that.

I pointed to myself, saying, "Mommy. I'm Mommy. Can you say that?"

He stood quiet, then picked up his bottle, sucking on it for a while, then crying again. I kissed his sweaty forehead, then turned on the Big Bird night-light.

"Goodnight, Sweetheart," I said, and switched off the ceiling light and headed out the door. I stood there, deciding whether it was OK to leave him alone.

After a while, I went downstairs, where Keith was leaning into the fridge, helping himself to spinach lasagna in the kitchen. "This is good stuff," he said with a mouthful, putting the lid back on the dish, sticking it back inside the fridge. "I didn't know you made that."

"I made it last night for your kids, remember? You had that thing to go to."

"Well, it's pretty darn good." He put the spoon in the sink along with the other dirty dishes I'd left out from supper. He reached for my hand and I gave it to him, and then he pulled me against him, leaning over and kissing my ear. "How's it going?" he whispered.

The first day I moved in, Keith asked me out, but I wasn't interested. After that, every time I left the place, he was outside doing something—washing the car, playing Frisbee or just sitting on the front step with his kids. Sometimes he mowed my lawn. We left for work at the same time, pulling out of the drives, waving goodbye like the stupid Brady Bunch. His girls were always knocking on my door, asking me to play. I figured maybe they missed their mother, whom they hadn't seen since the divorce. Keith didn't seem to mind doing it all himself, but things were different for me—I was still getting used to living alone, no Scotty, myself and Ian to take care of, and in England to boot, though I guess that didn't matter so much since I never went anywhere off base, so it was like a tiny America there. I sat around a lot, staring at Ian, thinking about calling Scotty, wondering if I'd done the right thing in leaving.

At the base in the middle of Nowhere England, I worked at the clinic that was connected to a kind of bunker that had been a morgue in the Second World War. I wore combat boots and BDUs. I checked in patients, took their vital signs, and did blood work when Doctor Frye ordered it. It was just the two of us and not a lot to do, so I spent a lot of time plunking away at an old abandoned piano in the bunker. Keith worked in supply, over at the warehouse, a big place with a lot of room, where he got good at volleyball. When stuff did come in, he and his friends inventoried stuff that everyone on base said was supposedly a secret.

While I worked, Ian stayed with an Air Force wife who had a British accent. Keith's daughters went to a pretty girl named Judy.

Scotty had been there, at that base in England, during Desert Storm. He was a medic, like me, and helped set up a war hospital in one of its giant hangers, waiting for casualties. Though none of them were sent there. I was in New Jersey on the blood collection team, processing units to freeze up for a stockpile.

After that so-called war, Scotty came home, left the Air Force, and beat me into a wall. Then the Air Force gave me orders for England, which seemed to me a convenient way to get away.

After I got set up in England, I cleaned up the administrative mess left over from the war: old papers, charts and scattered schedules. When I went to the base bank to set up an account, an Irish teller named Geri saw my name—she asked if I'd known Scotty—she was the first person there I met who'd known him. After I told her he was my soon-to-be ex-husband, she got quiet, nodding, saying she was sorry. But she was real friendly after that, anytime I stepped into the bank to cover the bad checks Scotty wrote me. Once she invited me over for tea, and although I told her I didn't want to see it, she showed me a videotape of a birthday party for Scotty she'd had at her house. Something he hadn't mentioned. She fast-forwarded the tape, showing sections of the tape where Scotty slammed Guinness while playing Spades and cussing. It wasn't his best performance. The people on the tape were all strangers to me.

After I went home and put Ian into bed, I started thinking about all that stuff with Scotty. I knocked on Keith's door and asked what he was doing.

Keith and I ate together most nights, and while we did the dishes, the kids would play or watch Barney or some Disney movie. After we put the kids to bed, we'd sit outside or in front of the TV. The British girls that I'd seen going to Keith's weren't visiting anymore, and his daughters started asking if I was going to be their mother. On the weekends, we'd get the teenage babysitter whose parents worked on base, and Keith and I would drive around looking at all the buildings constructed with local stone. That was kind of like the only tourist attraction there was. Sometimes we'd drive to the nearest village and eat at Indian restaurants, then stop at little pubs to drink half pints of cider. It was a pleasure spending time with a guy who seemed to have some idea of a life that could be more complex than most of the men I'd known. One Saturday, we drove to the nearest station, then took the train to London, where we got lost in the Underground, although that didn't matter much, because wherever it stopped, we got off, and there were things to do. We took pictures at Big Ben, Buckingham Palace and Piccadilly Circus. Then it rained and we'd forgotten our umbrellas, so we sat in the park, watching drops fall in the water, laughing at one another in our dripping summer clothes. When it finally stopped, we went to a souvenir shop and bought big London towels and oversized red T-shirts and found a fitting room, where we kissed and touched playfully while undressing one another. We dried each other off, then put on our new clothes, stuffing our wet ones inside the plastic bag, which we forgot, not noticing we'd left anything behind until hours had gone by.

When we got home, we reported everything to the babysitter and the kids, like newlyweds returning from a honeymoon. And for the first time in years I thought I might be in love with someone, but I wasn't about to be the first one to say it—I was waiting for him.

Stuff was going on in the world, but I never paid attention. So when a hospital in Germany needed extra help because of the ethnic war in Bosnia, it caught me by surprise. The doctor and I suddenly got temporary orders. We'd be there for a couple months, which meant Ian couldn't come with me, something in the military I was supposed to be prepared for. There wasn't time to send Ian to the States to stay with Scotty, so I got him ready to stay behind with Keith, then packed my bags and shined my boots, and got on the big C5.

I worked the lab. The first few days I read procedure manuals like ones I'd read before. I opened the books and stared at the pages, thinking about Ian and Keith. I already knew the drill, but the boss wanted me to refresh, so I made an effort. About the third day in, this Mike guy came up, rolled his chair beside me. His rank was sergeant, same as me. "You want a break?" he said. "They're doing a procedure in the back if you want to watch."

I looked up at his cocked thin eyebrows that looked like they'd been penciled in with magic marker. He took me to the room in the far back corner of the lab, by the histology department. As we got closer, the scent got stronger, a combination of the fresh blood like I'd collected while on the blood collection team, formalin, and the dead chickens my grandmother used to butcher.

He opened the heavy silver door and we went in. A dead guy lay on the table—he was young, reminded me of Scotty, big and muscular. His arms were stiff and a tag was tied to his right toe. A big cut split his chest, and the skin was peeled back like a life-sized Fruit Roll Up. Gashes made huge dimples on his legs. The penis leaned limp to one side. Two guys in scrubs and gloves held knives, scooping out the insides. Mike introduced us, but I didn't register their names. "Guy was in Bosnia and got busted with a load of shrapnel, so they sent him here with all the others. They did surgery and he coded on the table," Mike said.

I stared at the corpse, inhaled the smell, watching the two men in scrubs dissect the body and throw the dead man's remains into an enormous plastic bucket.

I started thinking too much, then the two scrubbed men cut the scalp open and peeled it back as if it were some mask you'd wear for Halloween. After I saw the skull, I closed my eyes. I wanted to see Keith. I wanted to hold Ian. I wanted to live the best life that I could. I kept staring as the two pathologists laughed and told jokes and cracked the soldier's dead white bones.

"Are you ready to go?" Mike said. "You look a little pale."

"I'm fine," I said.

"They've been coming in now and then. We're really short-handed. Glad you're here, cause when they fly in all messy, they need a lot of labs."

I stared at the manuals for the rest of the day, wondering if the dead soldier had a wife and kids, if his parents were alive, what his life was like, if he enlisted knowing he would die. I called Keith that night, and nothing there had changed—he told the kids to turn the volume down. Then I called Scotty. He told me that he missed me.

When I got back to England, Keith was dating a new girl, Justine, who worked for the commander. She was 22, had thin long hair and big teeth like Bugs Bunny. She was sick a lot, always at the clinic. Keith and I kept seeing each other, having dinner and family nights, and sex, just like we were married, and the two of them were only dating here and there, which I wasn't happy about, but I didn't want to let him go. One day while she was in the clinic, she needed a white count for some infection she suspected she might have. I didn't ask her about it, just donned a pair of gloves and put the needle in her arm, but she had tiny veins so I had to dig around. I finally hit something, and watched the tube fill up with blood.

I looked up, and saw Justine fanning her face with her free hand. She looked a little pasty, and I had enough blood for what I needed, so I popped the tourniquet, withdrew the needle and covered the venipuncture site with gauze, then threw the needle in the biohazard can. I grabbed an ammonia capsule so I could wake her if she fainted.

"You don't look so hot," I said.

"Oh, I'm fine," she said, leaning her elbows on her knees, lowering her head.

"That didn't happen last time," I said, taking off my gloves.

"It only happens when the needle moves around."

"Sorry. You have little veins."

"It's OK," she said, sitting upright. "I'm better now. Maybe you could take me back to the place everyone talks about? The old morgue. Everybody says it's real creepy."

"It's nice and cool and quiet," I said.

I handed her a Band-Aid, then opened the biohazard fridge and put her blood in a rack that waited to be sent away. I removed my lab coat and hung it over a chair. After she got some color, we washed our hands, then passed Doctor Frye's office and found him staring out the window. I nodded to him and said I was taking Justine to the bunker.

I opened the double doors that lead to a long descending hallway. It wound around and finally led us to two more double doors that were always hard to open and creaked as I pulled the handles. I flipped on the lights and we went inside. Old boxes sat on dusty litters and dim lights shook and flickered. We passed stacks of old medical equipment: dental chairs and patient tables, inpatient beds piled up with crutches that were probably never used. Old-fashioned wheelchairs sat unfolded along one wall, like they were still waiting to carry casualties away. Cobwebs lurched over them and hung from one piece of equipment to the next. We walked to the far end, to the piano, the only thing in the place that was somewhat clean. I'd been playing it almost every day, so I kept it free of dust. I even polished it sometimes.

"I would never come here all alone," Justine said.

She struggled with a few short tunes on the piano, and then I took over. She walked around, looking a little nervous. "Can I ask you something?" she said.

I said, "Uh-huh" and hit the middle C.

"Does Keith get around? What I mean is, well, does he sleep around a lot?"

I said, "Why would you ask?"

Suddenly we got busy at the clinic. It seemed as though everyone needed lab work. Monday it was Geri from the bank. I hadn't seen her for months. She sat in the phlebotomy chair and asked how I was doing.

"Great!" I said, looking at the slip checked HIV while she pulled up her sleeve.

"I never see you anymore," she said. "You still getting a divorce?"

I uncapped the needle. "I hope so," I said. I put the needle into her arm and she jumped a little.

"Dan and I are divorcing, too. Seems like it's going around. I guess it's just the military." Her Irish accent suddenly seemed extra strong. "Military marriages don't last. It's my second one. Next time I'll know better."

That night Keith asked Justine to marry him. I knew right away, because Justine came over after he'd given her the ring, saying she wanted me to be the first to know. It was an ugly diamond. I was holding Ian and he giggled at her cheery voice. I smiled and told her that was just the greatest thing. After she went home and Ian was in bed, Keith came over, telling me he was relieved because he didn't get rejected.

"Why isn't Justine staying with you tonight?" I said. "Seems like you two would want to celebrate."

"She wants to wait until after the wedding before having sex with me," he said.

I thought about how dumb that sounded—I'd been that way with Scotty. I stared down at Scotty's watch, which I'd started wearing, and laughed a little bit. "That's kind of sweet," I said. I stood there for a minute, thinking about Keith's ex-wife, about Scotty, about Dan and Geri, about the stuff she said had happened. I looked up and saw Keith's glow, his cloudy eyes, his stupid face. I grabbed his hand and lead him to my bedroom. I took off all our clothes, and kissed him gently on the lips.

After it was over, he got up and opened the blinds and stared down out the window. The streetlight lit the room. Then Keith got back in bed and lay next to me, staring at me the way he always did after we had sex. "I really like you, you know," he said, brushing my bangs to one side. He kissed my lightly, brushing his lips across my forehead, then got up again and gathered his clothes, and I watched him put them on. He patted my hand, then walked toward the doorway. When he turned to look at me, I closed my eyes, pretending not to see, then I listened to him trailing down the stairs.

After I knew he was gone, I went down and locked the door, came back upstairs, put on my robe and checked on Ian, watching him sleep in the slatted light from the street. He looked just like his father. I thought about calling Scotty. I tried to imagine what I'd say.

FORMATION

The technical instructor sang a cadence: *uu, oo, ee, our*. Little consonants were needed. The airmen had been in training for three days, and they could march, swing their arms, and turn when they heard a column right.

The tallest airman was the front and right of the formation. The shortest was the back and left. The others were between. They were all in order. They almost looked alike, except for their sizes.

There was Minnie, Ruby, Scarlet. Sara, Betsy, Janet. Jill, and Kit, and Penny. They were all there for some reason.

The instructor commanded them to halt. They did, but not in unison. It was like a football game, the wave, which a girl named Stacy knew about so well. Her brother was a Packer.

The instructor yelled for them to get it right.

Last night, in their beds they lay, the beds aligned in perfect rows. The blankets were green and the pillows were small and some pillows were wet. Some of the airmen had been crying. Some of them stared up at the walls, listening to the dripping of the sink, ready to jump.

Now they stood in formation. Trying to act.

POOL PARTY

Gretchen and Amy and I pedaled our bikes down the side street single file, our hair flying as we sped through the green light, coasting down a small hill that would take us past the railroad tracks where we would take a left, to Matt Bunker's house, who had been dating Amy since meeting her last weekend.

Bunker was tall and almost sixteen, with brown hair, green monster eyes and a smile that was electric. His bright teeth were almost as shiny as his silvery eyes. Playing football and baseball, and being the wrestling champion made his muscles hard and smooth.

At night, Amy and Gretchen and I went to Visions, the local teenage dry bar, where we would try to look our best, hoping to find nice boys to dance with, in hopes of being their girlfriends. Sometimes before we went there, we'd drink berry wine coolers at Amy's older sister's.

Friday night Bunker asked Amy to dance, and later they left for a walk. She told me they went to the woods and sat on a log, mosquitoes nipping their ankles, and she let his hand slip under her skirt—she said it was the first time any boy had moved his fingers inside her like that. He asked her to go steady, so she let him do what he wanted. He left two hickeys on the back of her neck. After that, he walked her to the curb.

Now Gretchen and Amy and I rode over the railroad tracks. Bunker called Amy the day before and invited her to the pool party, giving her directions, telling her to bring friends.

Bottled water sloshed in my bag, where my towel was folded. Amy's yellow towel rested over her shoulder. She said that Bunker had cute friends. She sped in his driveway. Gretchen and I rode behind.

"What if they don't like me?" Gretchen asked.

"Don't be silly," Amy said. "Bunker likes me, and you're prettier."

"Am not."

"Guys are always asking for your number."

"Of course they'll like us. If they don't, we'll leave," I said, getting off my bike.

"Don't be so confident. It'll ruin you someday," Amy said, turning to me, asking me to retie the top string of her bikini.

Bunker opened the front door, and asked what we were doing.

"She's tying up my suit. You wanna do it instead?" Amy winked.

He invited us inside. We left our bikes standing in the driveway.

The sun was hot that day. After Bunker let us inside, he offered us a beer. We chose Bud Light Ice.

We all went to the back yard, where Bunker's friends sat outside in lawn chairs getting stoned, sucking on small rolled-up sheets of paper, closing their eyes and holding in their breaths. Then they finally exhaled.

Bunker introduced everyone. His friends were Nate and Darren. One nudged the other and smiled. Gretchen giggled. I waved to Bunker and he turned his chin up.

Bunker and Amy went back inside, and Gretchen and I sat on the edge of the pool, dipping our feet in the water, holding our beers. Darren and Nate sat around the table, sucking on their paper. They took off their shirts. Then a guy named Angel came over—he had dark hair and blue eyes. He joined the others at the table. After another beer, Gretchen and I sat with them. The boys smoked their pot. We took a couple drags, coughing.

Outside, the three boys sat around the pool and Gretchen and I stripped down to our suits. Gretchen's bikini was pink with white flowers, and it made her look good and skinny. Mine was neon orange with blue stripes. I tried to suck in my stomach. Everyone held bottles.

The boys talked about football players and training camp, while Gretchen whispered to me that she thought Nate was handsome.

We smiled, watching the boys. I said Angel was cute.

We sunk our feet in the water, moving them in circles.

"What are you girls doing all summer?" Nate said.

"Hanging around, I guess." Gretchen said. She crossed her legs and took a sip of beer.

"We usually go to Ashwaubomay," I said.

"We were there all last summer before Bunker got the pool. Funny we didn't see you," Darren said.

The boys looked at each other. Gretchen and I blew in our bottles, making whistling sounds.

After Gretchen and I finished another beer, we got up and went inside and threw our empty bottles in the trashcan. The glass made clanging noises.

"Let's get in the pool," Gretchen said.

I said, "I think I'm getting tipsy."

In the kitchen, Amy found us, getting more beer.

We joined the boys. The gray-haired neighbor waved to us and we waved back, then jumped into the deep end. We came up for air, treading water. We all swam laps, then sat on the edges, drinking beer and talking. Bunker sat by Amy, putting a hand on her knee. I sat by Angel, and Nate shared a beer with Gretchen. Darren sat alone until two other guys came to join the party. The neighbor peered over the fence while everyone got wasted.

People splashed around, and the couples got mixed up. Bunker put his hand under my bikini when Amy wasn't watching. I tried to move away, but then Angel came and joined him. I kicked and screamed, and Gretchen and Amy tried to help me, but then the other boys held them, doing the same to them. It was a big commotion.

The boys lifted our legs up around their hips while we

screamed and kicked and flailed. I half-laughed, as if it were a joke.

The boys hooted and cheered and took turns sliding their hands under the elastic of our bottoms, fingering us. The neighbor watched, sipping his Blue Ribbon.

After it was over, Gretchen and I went inside and found Amy in the bathroom.

"I can't believe him," Amy said. "I really thought I loved him."

Gretchen held her. Amy asked if we were all right.

"We're fine," I said. "They didn't hurt you, did they?"

I tried to hide my scratches. After Amy saw them, she rummaged through Bunker's cabinet, looking for Band-Aids.

"It's OK," I said. "I'm fine."

"Yeah, they were only playing," Gretchen said, blotting a cut of her own.

We all went back outside, where Bunker popped his Bud and Amy turned her back to him. Gretchen and I dried ourselves with our towels.

"You guys ready?" Amy grabbed her bag.

"I guess." Gretchen put her clothes over her suit. We put our bags over our shoulders. Gretchen and I waved to the boys, then said, "See ya later."

Alongside one another, we rolled our ten-speeds down the driveway.

"When we going back?" Gretchen said.

"Never," Amy said. "I can't believe what happened."

We rode in silence. We went to the nearest stop sign, where we took a break, laying our bikes across the grass. We sat on a bench inside a dirty bus stop shelter.

"I think I'm bleeding inside," Gretchen said.

"I gave him a blow job," Amy said.

"Don't worry," I said.

"It wasn't that bad," Gretchen said, squeezing her own shoulder.

We sat there for a while. A blue transit bus roared, then stopped to pick us up. Amy waved it on. An old man with a beard and long gray hair peered at us through his window. It was dusty. The driver pushed up his glasses. Then the bus rolled off. A noise sighed from the exhaust. Its fumes were filthy gray and potent.

"What's for tomorrow?" Amy said.

"Ashwaubomay?" Gretchen said.

I told them we'd figure out something.

We rode ahead, the wind blowing on our misty doll-like faces.

HOPE TOWN

I tell my mom: the menu offers frog legs. Still hoping to win over her affection. I'm in another state, New York, at home with an infection.

I was supposed to have taken a trip today with my boyfriend to help his dad build a shed kind of like a doghouse. I woke up peeing blood though.

There is no menu. No busboy, no lawn chairs to speak of.

My sweetheart left without me.

I spent hours in the ER.

When I tell my mom I love to sleep outside, she says, what if someone rapes you?

THE MEAT PLACE

I'm driving my aunt Sarah's Lexus, taking us to the meat place. We pass farms with pastures full of Holsteins and green trees. Weeds fill the ditches. Beyond in the woods are deer, raccoons and skunks. Sometimes, driving on the road, I see them try to cross. Sometimes I see a carcass.

I used to see these fields, living on a farm nearby. Then my parents divorced and I moved to town with my mother. I was fifteen and it was a hard time for me. When we'd drive back to the old place, I'd look out at the fields, my body feeling like a graveyard, hardly thinking what was out there.

That's when my aunt and I got close. She lived in town, and would ask me to come over, paying me to vacuum. I'd clean the toilets, scrub the mirrors and dust. Sometimes she gave me money to go shopping, saying to get her husband Harry white cotton shirts in extra-larges, and for her, maybe a sweatshirt. I'd always give her the receipts, and she'd hand me a ten or twenty that I might put away later so I could buy myself a sweater. I'd use some of it for lunch. My mom had filed for assistance, so at school I was supposed to get free meals, but I was too embarrassed and never used the tickets.

I still feel the weight of the memory of that time. I stay in the slow lane, letting cars pass, and I try to focus on the highway. Most of the cars are domestic—that's what most of us drive here in the great Midwest. Semis whiz like storms. Then one semi crosses over to my lane. I try to press the horn. I hear nothing so I scream. I jerk onto the shoulder.

My aunt holds onto the door. She points and says, "The horn's there in the middle."

She says, "It's only fifty-five here, but I go a little faster."

We are just outside the city, almost to the place where local farmers and hunters take their poultry, veal and beef. Before my uncle Harry got sick, he'd kill his deer, butcher them and skin them. He'd bring whatever was left to the meat place.

When I was a kid, my family hired a butcher to slaughter our own cows, ones too old for milking. It's just how things happened. Then when I turned eight, I was put in charge of wrapping. I remember the feel of the warm meat, folding it with paper, sealing it with tape and writing whatever part I was told it was with the fat black pen that smelled like glue and copper: sirloin, ground round, cube steak, tail and heart and tongue. After I was done, I'd put them in a giant cooler, and then my mom kept track of things on a pad of yellow paper.

She'd talk to the butcher, saying things like, "Sorry my daughter's so slow. She's a little Cinderella."

My mother would tell me to speed up. Hearing that would send me trying to wrap faster, but then I'd forget what I just wrapped, having to unwrap again so I'd label it correctly. That only frustrated her more, and she'd say things to me like, "Your father will be mad. We'll be late for supper."

My dad was always off doing all his own stuff: plowing, planting corn, maybe cleaning stanchions or helping a cow with a delivery, wrapping a rope around a newborn's slimy hooves once the calf started to emerge—he'd use most of his strength to try to pull. If the calf was born a bull, he never kept it. He only kept the heifers, since they'd eventually be milking, and that's where my father made his profit. He hired breeders from a place called Midwest Breeders.

My dad ordered semen from a catalogue and he would lock the in-heat cow into a stanchion. Then the breeder arrived, bringing his boots, his apron, his long-sleeved gloves, his case. I wasn't allowed to watch the rest. My dad would say, "Go away. You don't need to see this."

The breeder was always the same guy. I called him Mister Gene. We belonged to the same church and his son James was in my class. James was the first boy I had a crush on—we'd send each other notes under our desks, saying things like, "I really like you." He left me squares of Bubble Yum, and we held hands once on the bus.

When James would be in the car, I'd go out and hope to see him. I'd be doing chores like feeding the calves an extra bale of hay, or combing one with the brush to get her ready for the fair. James was in 4-H like me—at the fair we showed cows and heifers. There weren't a lot of bulls there.

At home in the basement, my family had two gigantic freezers, with all different kinds of meat and organs—I thought this kind of thing was common until I started talking about it with my friends as an adult. I never questioned it until my friends seemed alarmed to hear I ate my favorite cow, Iona. I loved that cow. When I fed her weeds under the fence, she always let me pet her.

Now in the car, my aunt says, "Look, a buck," pointing to the woods. I see her hands, all veined and thin, and since her cancer diagnosis months before, her psyche has gone shaky.

"Where?" I say.

"Over there," she says. "Maybe we should get Harry some venison or sausage."

I say, "He wanted the ground round."

I've been cooking non-stop for my aunt and uncle. I flew in last week from New York. I haven't been here in two years. I don't like coming back, but they're in bad shape and I feel like I have to do something.

I try to cook low in fat, since my uncle Harry's heart thing and then his complications. Two months after his attack, he went in for surgery to have a stent replaced, only to be rushed back that night to the ER when he couldn't stop throwing up and bleeding. One, two, three, all those days, I'd call him on his cell phone from New York, hearing beeping, the alarm of an IV, a lab tech in to draw his blood work. I could hear him chattering in the background, saying "Another stick?" then "No, it doesn't hurt much."

"I hope you're in good hands," I'd say.

When I'd say, "Where is Aunt Sarah?" he'd say, "Oh, she's back at home. She hasn't been so well. She won't tell me much. Yesterday Shirley stopped over and found her passed out in the hallway."

Shirley is their friend. She's stressed from keeping track of them.

The day before I came, she said, "I can't be there all the time."

I said, "You don't have to be. Why should you?"

She said, "I really shouldn't. I have to take care of my own life."

Now my aunt hardly eats, sometimes curled over saying, "Fuck," there's a hiccup in her backbone, her stomach an explosion. She says, "Fuck the pain. This fucking pain!"

And then she'll take some pills: the Oxy or the Lexapro or Xanax, or the estrogen blocker with the complicated name that's supposed to stop the spreading of her cancer. She shouldn't be drinking. She was a drinker before her cancer, but after her diagnosis, she started drinking daily. Since I've been here she's snuck out twice to get pints of vodka, slamming as much as possbile before making it home again.

The last time, after she woke, as she staggered and fell into the wall, I asked, "Are you hung over?" She leaned and asked me, "How'd you know?"

She's only sixty-five and she shouldn't be this sick yet.

She's the same age as Harry and my mom. They all went to high school together. My mom is somewhere with a new guy on vacation and isn't here to help. My dad's been dead two years. It was a suicide, part of his mental illness even though he was living in a place where people came three times a day to check on him and give him medication. One day a social worker found him hanging in the bedroom—my aunt called me with the news, leaving a message on my voicemail.

We pass a store where my dad used to get things for his farm—stuff like welding hats and shovels, nails, and tools to burn off horns of heifers. I remember going with him. Though I'm not sure why, my mother said I had to. I'd ride shotgun in his truck, looking out the window, holding my lips shut, afraid something would set off my dad and he'd start yelling. When he got to the lot, I followed him in. As he paced the aisles, I tried to lag behind him. He never said what he was doing. The building had high ceilings and a cement floor, and things were stacked in crates and boxes. It smelled like manure and rust.

Passing by the store, I say to my aunt, "That's where my dad used to get his farm stuff."

I want to ask her what it was like to grow up with my dad, if he played with trains, or if he had a thing for swing sets. People say my baby pictures look like his. As a boy, he had big eyes and long lashes. Some pictures show him in his barn clothes. The older he gets, the more his face gets stoic. Looking through the albums I never find the mean face I was scared of. I don't know who he was. He was fit and handsome, like people on TV. He had thick blond hair with a cowlick above the left side of his forehead.

I keep trying to ask my aunt things about her life as a child, what my dad was like, if there were signs and problems. When I first got here again this time, when I asked those things she said, "I don't remember." She got up and said, "How 'bout some wine?" She poured and poured. She slipped me hundred-dollar bills, and I wanted to ask again about my dad, but I knew by then she'd probably forgotten.

"Are you OK?" I say as we near the meat place. My aunt looks a little antsy.

She says to me, "Pull up," pointing to a station.

I prepare to sit and wait. I watch her clutch her purse and open the door. People go in and out in Packer shirts and John Deere hats, but also men in ties, women wearing blazers. I turn on the air. A man leans on his Ford, bouncing a toddler in diapers. His thick hair and pretty smile remind me of my boyfriend Brad who calls me everyday when he's walking my Chihuahua.

So I call him. After our hellos, I ask him, "Did you run?"

He says to me, "Not yet."

I picture his green eyes. It was the first thing I noticed when we met for a run around the park next to the zoo, where you can see the giraffes' necks if you look in the right places. That day I heard an elephant, a roar. We ran that loop three times, talking about hill repeats and getting shoes stuck in the mud when running trails and competing in cross-country.

He says, "Are you OK?"

I say to him, "I think I am. I will be."

He says, "I know it's hard."

I say, "It's probably good I came."

He says to me, "I know."

He's been listening to me struggle. When I first heard about the return of my aunt's cancer, I cried on his bare skin, and he just stayed there and he held me.

We went to the zoo, where he took my hand. We looked at the giraffes. We bought peanuts and fed them to the elephants, watching them move their trunks like Slinkys. We watched the monkeys swing, and heard their sounds like coughing. My eyes felt red, and my insides felt like soppy rag that was getting a good cleansing.

Still, I don't expect Brad to know what it's like for me to be here. I like his mom, his dad, his sister and her kids. They have me over and ask me how I am. They set a plate for me, and ask if I want seconds. They offer me dessert. They say there is no pressure.

I look at the dash and see a blinking light. It's circular and red. I say, "It's good I'm here."

He says, "I really miss you."

I say, "I miss you too," looking at the console. I think my aunt's been inside a while, though I'm not sure how many minutes.

"Sugarplum," he says. "I have to walk the dogs now."

After we hang up, I push a button, trying to find music. I find a station where a woman's voice is singing about rainbows. It reminds me of my mother humming to the radio on our way to church as my father drove his Silverado. The one time I leaned ahead and asked to change the channel, my mother said, "Stay quiet with your lips tight. You'll make your father happy."

She started saying that a lot. It took me a while to realize that meant my father didn't want to be bothered. After that I started to bite my lips so hard they were always bleeding.

I start getting thirsty, so when I see my aunt's bottled water in the holder, I reach for it and sip. This one is water. This morning I gave her a water bottle filled with vodka. The first couple days I tried to stop her. Each morning I was there, she'd pace and fidget with her keys, saying she had to run an errand: get things like mineral water, milk, and she got me Starbucks coffee. She'd leave just before eight: the time places in Wisconsin can start selling liquor.

Sometimes she'd leave earlier, but she wouldn't come back until sometime after eight. One time she left around six, said she had to get lettuce from the grocer, and after she left my uncle said, "She sometimes drinks vanilla extract."

She'd come home and then pass out until it was time for more. I tried to understand her pain. I was pretty sure she'd die soon.

Then Harry took her keys. I wasn't sure what to do then, but I decided I couldn't stop her. She's hurting and she's scared. This might be all she has now. So last night I bought a pint of vodka and a large bottle of water. I drank that water, slamming the whole thing, remembering how water is supposed to flush you. I poured the vodka in the bottle. I got up three times that night and peed, then after I woke at six a.m., I sat in the living room, not knowing what to do yet, but I sat there with the bottle full of vodka--then when she came around, pacing, up the stairs, then down, she asked me where her keys were. I said, "Harry doesn't want you driving."

Her shoulders dropped, and it seemed the rest of her just followed. She nodded and she said to me, "OK."

I sat there for a while. I heard and watched her pace. When I sensed her in the kitchen, I got up and went there and I handed her the bottle. I said, "It isn't water."

As she took a sip, her eyes glowed.

"Whoa!" she said. "I thought that was water."

I said to her, "I'm sorry. I don't know what to do." I felt a little shaky.

She hugged me and she said, "That's OK." She hugged me again and she said, "Thank you."

Now when she comes out of the station, I can't tell if she looks calm or if she's shaky. When she gets in, I sit a while and say, "Did you get rid of the evidence?"

She says, "How'd you know?"

I was there when Harry found the empty half-pint in her purse. He showed it to her. He asked her, "What is this?" and after she sat up and staggered to the bathroom, he said to me, "How can we ever stop her?"

I said, "We can't. She's frightened and in pain. It's the only thing that helps her."

He said, "But she says she wants to stop. I've told her that I've had it. I can't be with her when she's like this."

Now she hugs her purse and says, "I only drank half of it."

As I drive across the lot to the meat place, I say, "Do you want me to go in?"

She opens her door and says, "Yes, let's," and on the way in, she hands me a bunch of crumpled hundreds. I see her heading to the bathroom, taking small quick steps that remind me of my grandma. My aunt wears a cap to cover her bald spots. Her pants are the same from days before: baggy, matching the oversized university sweatshirts from the supply she gets from the outlet.

I look through the glass cases that seem endless: rows of steaks and pork and chicken. It turns my gut to be here. Venison and sausages and cheese. I take a number from the machine that says to take a number. Mine says 54. A man from behind the counter wearing white calls out number 50. Other customers look through glass like I do. I can tolerate the cooking of the meat and I can eat it, but I hate seeing the slabs behind the case—it's as if they're lost pieces to a puzzle.

I want to leave. I walk up and down, waiting for my number. I focus on a blonde girl wearing pink who puts her tongue onto the case until a fat man lifts her. I see bacon, ham. The place smells like jam and mud. I finally hear a 54, then point to the lean ground round.

On the way home, we go through roundabouts, returning. They are new, with construction cones like carrots. My aunt looks calm. She turns the radio up. "Thank you," she says. I like this car, with its fancy button. You just press it and it starts as long as the keys are in it. The doors won't lock with the keys in it either. It's Krupp-proof, my aunt told me. She and I, we're Krupps. We make crumbs and are forgetful. We lose things. We can't find our direction.

Nearing the city again, we come up to the stoplight where, at fifteen, I got hit. I was on my bike. It was sprinkling, dark. I was wearing a white sweater and baggy pinstriped pants. I remember lying on the pavement. Staring at the sky. I remember being peaceful.

My aunt says, "Do you think anything is up there?"

I say, "I don't know. I hope so."

She says, "Besides sky?"

I say, "I believe everyone is something. Self-responsibility, integrity, compassion. I know it. I believe."

She says, "My dad was such a bastard. I hated how he preached at us. I got tired of his god talk."

I say, "He used to make me feel important."

She says to me, "You *are*."

I say, "I used to think I loved him."

I've told her this before. After my parents divorced, since my father was so sick and suicidal, there was no question I'd be living with my mother. Then one day after school, my grandfather came over with my grandma. I was there alone—my dad was in the barn and my mother was getting things set up in the new place. My grandpa said, "You should be living with your father."

I was scared of my father. I knew I didn't want to live with him.

My grandpa said, "He needs you." I didn't know what to say. He said, "You're a sinner. You'll be damned. I no longer have a grandchild." Then I watched him take my grandma's hand, head out the door, and back out of the driveway.

My aunt says, "Yeah, I know."

I hear sirens so I pull off to the side. An ambulance speeds by.

Back on the road I say, "I don't want you to suffer. Tell me what to do."

My hands sweat at the wheel. She says, "I just want you here. I think you understand. You're so unlike Shirley. She acts like my mother."

I remember calls to Shirley weeks before I came. She could go on and on. I say, "She's not sure what to do. She cares for you. She's scared."

My aunt says, "So am I. I'm not sure I trust my doctor."

The wheel is sticky. I brake so hard my neck hurts.

I say to her, "Why not?"

"He's lying. I can feel it."

"Why would he lie?"

"He doesn't do anything to help."

I say, "Don't skip any more appointments. Tell him you need more for pain. Maybe you should be telling things like this to Harry."

"He just wants to interfere."

"He wants to be a part. You have to let him in. He's taking it personally."

When I'd call, he'd tell me she'd been at it. When she'd come to the phone, she'd mumble things like snow. I couldn't understand her. She might say, "I don't think they know what they're doing."

I'd call Shirley, who'd already tried to call the doc, the social worker, even the cops and legal people. One time she rang the doorbell, and when nobody answered, she went in and found my aunt dead-looking on the sofa. She went to the bed and woke my uncle. He tried to carry her. Shirley grabbed the phone. My aunt ended in ICU with an alcohol level hardly anyone has heard of.

But a time or two, she'd talk clearly and tell me of her treatment, about the estrogen blockers that are supposed to stop the spreading of her cancer. Once she said, "I hate them. They're a bitch."

I say, "Talk to Harry. It would help him if knew that."

I think of recent talks: before I came, he said, "She drove into the mailbox. So I took her keys, and the next night she walked a mile to the station. I didn't get a call from her until eight a.m. The cops found her in the ditch and she was in the psych ward." I still imagine her high up: again in the same psych ward where my dad went.

When Harry tried to tell me about his first attack, he said, "I touched my heart and fell. Everything went black and then the pain left. I woke when Sarah touched me." I was on my end of the phone, sitting at my desk. I closed my eyes. I wanted to reach out. He didn't seem old before that.

We're almost home. My aunt Sarah's head drops in the front seat, and as she nods herself to sleep, we pass the high school I attended, where I ran track, cross-country and cheered for the wrestlers. I'd walk to class each morning, late, having to stop at the office to pick up my detentions, my stomach growling, telling myself I can wait for lunch, where I would allow myself an apple or a handful of peanuts.

My aunt wakes, saying, "Did we get the meat?"

"Yes," I say, and then she giggles.

As we pass another station, she points and says, "Let's stop there." It's the same station where—when I was in high school—my friends and I would find some man outside to take our cash and get us Old Style, PBR, whatever was the cheapest.

I know she needs more alcohol. I say, "We better not." I hear a ring. I think I find the phone tab.

"Hello?" I realize it's my uncle.

He asks me, "Are you with her?"

I say, "You were sleeping when we left. We didn't want to disturb you."

"But is she OK?"

I look at her. Back to the phone I say, "She's OK. We got your meat. The lean stuff."

He says, "I like it fresh and raw."

I tell him, "I remember."

I look at my aunt again, her head against the window. I turn back to the phone. "You holding up?" I say.

He says, "I'm about to mow the lawn."

I imagine him falling. Blades. "That's not a good idea," I say. "Let me. I need to do something."

I like to mow the lawn—it was my job when I was on the farm, and I'd ride all day on the tractor, up the hills and down them, going fast around the trees, speeding up as I was edging closer.

"I'll go slow," he says. "I need to."

As I turn onto the street, I nudge my aunt, say, "Sarah."

She turns to me, says, "Hey!" She laughs. She giggles. She mumbles something about Mars and she asks me if we're there yet.

At the house, my uncle sits on a lawn chair in the driveway, wearing shorts and some university T-shirt. He's sweating. I wave to him and pull in the garage, and say to my aunt, "We're here now."

She holds onto the car and walks around it. I grab her arm and help her up the stairs. When I say, "Are you OK?" she gives me the smile that I saw in my dad once.

I tell Harry, "I'll be back," and I take my aunt to her chair: brown and thick with cushion. It matches my uncle's. She sits and pulls the handle, which helps her put her feet up. She grabs my hand, says, "Thanks for understanding."

I say to her, "Sit tight," and I go out and find my uncle by the fence with a weed-whacker. He looks fatigued. His arms don't swing with the verve they did when he played all those years of baseball. He had a thing for golf. He was into those things before his knees went. He used to be muscular and strong: a hunter, going off to kill a bear. He even shot a moose once. He has antlers. Also trophies, now in boxes in the basement—he won tournaments in rugby. He served in Vietnam. After leaving the war, he started his own business. He works as an accountant.

A lot of their clients were small ones who thrived on winning seasons of the Packers. He's blocks from the stadium. He and my aunt have season tickets and once I went to a game with my aunt and Shirley, which was so much different from when I used to go in high school—then my friend Jan and I used to sit outside the stadium waiting for anyone to scalp. I was always cold, wearing shoes not meant for socks. We'd be in the stands and she'd point to this Packer player and then that one. I wasn't sure how all that worked but she'd tell me that she fucked them. When I went with my aunt and Shirley, we wore layers of green and walked there. We lifted ourselves and did the wave hardcore.

At the office, my aunt and uncle stocked the break room with stuff like fruit snacks and Little Debbies. Sausages and cheese. Mineral water and any kind of soda. My mom never had much food. We didn't have a lot of money. She wasn't around much, and when she was, she'd be with a different man, laughing in her room in the basement.

The office got really busy during tax time. My uncle would spend all his time there. He had his attack there. He was at his desk, two days before the IRS deadline.

Now I sit on the step and watch him working through a row. The lawn isn't thick. I mowed it the day after I got here and so far it's been a dry summer.

"You holding up?" I say. I'm tired from the effort. Since arriving, I've also been cleaning. Laundry and the dishes. Cooking and watering the plants. Hosing down the lawn, the trees, the flowers in the garden. Sorting through the mail and collecting calls from tenants living in my aunt and uncle's rentals.

He stays upright, walking to his lawn chair. "I feel great," he says. "I haven't moved in ages."

A truck turns in the driveway. "Hey, Hank," says my uncle, and as the man steps out, I remember him, a ranger at a sanctuary that preserves certain kinds of wildlife. He wears a camouflage hat, jeans, a shirt that says, "I'm for it."

"Hank," I say.

"Hey," he says. He turns his whole body towards my uncle. He says, "Our oldest skunk has died. I really learned to love him."

Harry puts his hand on his friend's shoulder and says, "Hank, remember you're a ranger."

I've been to the sanctuary before, seeing animals in cages. I went there on my own the day after my dad died. At first I didn't know why. It comforted me. I remember as a girl, talking to the cows and cats. I thought they always liked me.

I say, "Do you have any new ones? Animals, I mean?"

Hank says, "Today a badger had two pups. And a beaver had a kitten." He talks about the patterns of an owl, how the fledglings copy. He talks of ostriches and chicks. He says, "So Harry? When will we be hunting? I put up new stands on your land so we can study deer tracks."

Harry says, "Maybe in the fall. I'll be like new in no time."

I go inside, where my aunt lies back with her eyes closed. It's past ten a.m. I go to the guest room, where my things are, by the bed, though most nights I hardly get there—like at home, I fall asleep to the TV. I like to hear the voices.

I find my shoes, put on a running bra and shorts. I'm grateful for my iPod, a gift from my boyfriend who tells me I deserve things.

My aunt is still passed out. My uncle talks to Hank. "I'm going to run," I say.

Harry says, "As far as yesterday? And the day before?"

"I'm not sure," I say. "But you don't have to time me."

He laughs a little. Hank waves and I'm not sure what he says because I'm already up on volume.

I step down the street, deciding today I will go right, then left, then right again, passing the first place I moved to after my mother left my dad. Since then, I haven't seen it. I run fast, and out of breath, imagining how horrible it felt there. I still can envision when my mom said, "I don't need him," in the car and I how cried there, looking up at patterns in the ceiling. Everything whirled around. My parents never argued. I realized they didn't talk much.

I turn back and look at that old place, never knowing what I felt then. I run by the church lot where I had sex with my first boyfriend, where he first told me that he loved me. I remember hearing about James, the boy I liked when I was younger. He was the smartest in the class and I was second. Then in junior high, I learned from old friend he shot himself in a closet in his bedroom. He used his father's shotgun. I remember crying, wondering, sprinting laps around the track. I wished I'd saved his notes. I never really knew him. I go blocks to that old track. I pull on the gate. When I see that it is locked, I think of climbing over.

I run by the place where I got hit, remembering the accident, that big old sky, when I saw my bike in shambles.

Farther, there are dunes where I used to party with my friends in high school. We'd light a fire and sit on logs and pour keg beer into our cups, staying there until the cops came. I remember reaching for my mom. She had meetings and appointments. I remember running as a teen, how it always seemed to save me. I think about my aunt. I don't want her to go.

I see the fields. I run faster, going past them. The music is not new. I see green trees and grass and weeds. I go up a hill. I pump my arms and push my body to the top of it.

THE SCHUKERS' FOURTH OF JULY

The Girls' Room

Kate and Suzy Schuker lay in their bedroom talking of ways to kill their father. The eight-year-old twins prop their feet on pillows facing the head of the bed, and let their heads hang from its foot so their long hair skims the wooden floor. Kate slides her cow slippers on and off her feet and wiggles her toes. Suzy watches her own skin turn red as she looks at her features in the compact mirror: her fiery green eyes, bold freckles, and make-believe smile. She lets her pink-and-white polka-dot Drowsy doll, a hand-me-down from her older cousin, fall to the floor and. Suzy soundlessly criticizes her own appearance, wondering if her father would like her if she were more attractive.

Cupcakes

Janet, the twins' mother, sits on a varnished kitchen chair and talks on the phone to Yvonne, the overweight lady who lives two miles down the road. Janet laughs into the receiver as her black-bottom cupcakes bake in the gas oven. She makes them for a Ladies' Aid church event—the cupcakes make the house smell like a mixture of Hershey's candy bars and cutout Christmas cookies. She props her feet on a padded stool and stares at the cooking timer in her hand. The women talk about the upcoming Fourth of July celebration, the aftermath of the Columbine shootings, then Yvonne talks about her latest visit to the hairdresser, Mrs. Dee. Janet says, "Oh, really," "Uh huh," and "Yeah," as Yvonne tells her of the latest gossip. Janet wants to hear all about it.

Rubber Boots

Stanley's rubber boots make shuffling sounds on the concrete floor as he milks his cows. He cleans Tiny's udder with water from a hose with his callused hands, then puts the milkers on each teat, one at a time. He checks on his other three cows in the milking parlor and pulls the milkers from Sugar's udder and puts them on a metal rack. He opens the sliding door for Sugar to get out and when she doesn't move, he slaps her ribs with a wooden stick. "Stupid cow," he says. He lets the next one in.

Stanley mutters to himself as the milkers make sucking sounds and the milk makes whooshing sounds and the pipes carry the liquid to a big metal tank. He laughs to himself as he remembers a joke that his teammate, Alex told at a dartball game last night.

Stanley wipes his wet hands on his gray work pants, his fingers touching a place where manure splashed on a spot that was sticky from syrup. The muck lodges itself between the cracked callused parts of Stanley's hands that sometimes shake. Stanley doesn't notice.

Pancakes

This morning for breakfast the family ate pancakes. Janet made them big and dark for Stanley. Medium-sized light for the twins. Stanley put Mrs. Butterworth's on his, while the girls ate theirs with butter and Janet's strawberry jam. Janet took hers plain. They all drank milk that came from Stanley's cows.

Stanley got a Charlie horse and he grabbed his leg while it jerked. The table shook, spilling milk. Syrup dripped on Stanley's leg. Then everything was still.

Janet got up, cleaning up milk in places, wiping Mrs. Butterworth's from Stanley's gray pants. The twins chewed. They sat and stared. Then Stanley looked at them.

"What you two lookin at? You lookin at me?" His eyes veered away. He shook his head. "Damn." He looked at Janet. "Clean it up. Clean it all up. Get it off me. Get it all. That damn Butterworth. I told you to not to get that damn Butterworth."

"Sorry. I'll get it. I'll get it all cleaned up," Janet said.

"Damn bitch of a Butterworth." Stanley got up and stormed off, limping a little. He reached for the Mrs. Butterworth's bottle, took it outside and slammed it against the cement steps, breaking glass, leaving the stairs sticky in places. Then he went to the barn.

Janet cleaned up and the girls lost their appetites. Then the three recited the Lord's Prayer. It was something they always did after Stanley got mad.

The Girls' Room
"Maybe we can poison his food," Suzy sits up and puts down the mirror. She looks at Kate.

"What about the Ten Commandments?"

"Don't worry." Suzy gets up, finds her Drowsy doll and picks it up. "I know where the key to his gun cabinet is. I saw him shoot a skunk once. His guns look easy to use."

"Skunks are easy. They're dumb. Dad could be smart." Kate sits up, grabs her Mrs. Beasley doll (which Janet bought at the last antique rummage sale), and looks into the doll's plastic face. She thinks she looks like her doll, except for the hair.

"What do we do with him when he's dead?"

"I'm not doing it. I'm not going to hell." Kate pushes up her glasses.

"We have to do something," Suzy gets up and puts on her plastic necklace. She looks into the vanity next to the bed and puts on cherry lip gloss. She smacks her lips, imitating the way her mother looks into the mirror, turning her chin up and rotating it from left to right. Her red pigtails bounce.

"Let's face it. We're doomed." Kate's chin quivers and a tear rolls down her cheek, making her glasses wet. She hugs Mrs. Beasley.

Suzy gets out her drawing pad and draws a black flower.

Pansies

The Schukers' brick two-story is centered on the seven-acre lawn, a small part of the 80-acre farm. Ivy vines creep up the red brick, touching the roof. Purple lilac bushes, and a garden of pansies, daisies, and sunflowers mask the manure smell that sometimes looms when the wind blows from the east. Five oak trees bud.

A metal clothesline, white oil tank, and two barrels for burning waste sit in the back yard. In the front, white rocks make a trail, connecting the house to the gravel driveway, which separates the home from the barn, silo, manure pit, and other things needed for dairy-farm operations. The place is surrounded by nothing but fields, except for a narrow road, which forms a T with the gravel path. From this road, the home looks quaint and quiet, and everyone who passes by deems this a fact.

Yesterday

Stanley punished Suzy for running from the house to the barn naked. Suzy asked Janet why people needed to wear clothes. Janet told Suzy that if she wanted to find out, to run from the house to the barn in the nude—Janet didn't think Suzy really would.

Stanley was scraping manure from the heifers' stalls at the time, and he saw her. When Suzy saw him she ran back to the house. Stanley grabbed his stick from the barn, but he couldn't catch her—she was already out of sight.

Suzy ran to her room and crawled in bed. Janet saw what was coming so she locked the door, then went back to making monster cookies. Stanley banged on the door. Then kicked. Then took his stick and pounded some more. "Hey you, come back here. What you doing running around here like that? Around my barn. Around my cows. Around my yard."

Janet pretended not to hear, humming a tune.

Suzy shook under the sheets. Kate stood by the bedroom door. "At least you got away," she said.

"It's my damn house. My house. Let me in my damn house." Stanley yanked on the doorknob. His hands shook like wild. He took his stick, threw it on the ground, then sat on the front step banging his knees. Then he got up, picked up his pole and stormed to the barn. "My damn house," he said, talking to his cows.

Stanley slapped the stick, jabbing Maybell's ribs. "My damn house." Then he got Sharona. The rest of the cows hustled, kicking manure.

After it was quiet and Janet knew he was gone, she went upstairs. She saw Suzy shaking on the bed, Kate sitting by her side.

"I guess we got him in a bad mood. Sorry," Janet said, "But to answer your question: I'm not sure why people need clothes. It has to do with Adam and Eve." The twins shook their heads. Janet did too.

Then they said the Lord's Prayer.

"Mom, why is Daddy so mean?" Suzy asked.

"Well, like I said before, your dad gets grumpy from all his work. Things will get better, you'll see."

Suzy and Kate tried to believe.

Janet went downstairs and unlocked the door. The doorknob fell. Janet tried to fix it.

A Family

Stanley always lived there. After marrying Janet, his parents moved to a nearby town, leaving him to take over the farm. The newlyweds were happy together. Every night after Stanley finished milking the cows, and after Janet finished her household chores, they would stroll down the paths of the pastures. They would hold hands as Stanley led the way with his flashlight. They often stopped to look at the stars.

Stanley would talk about the plans for his crops and his herd, and Janet always listened. Then Stanley would tell his wife that he loved her and that he only wanted what was best for their future. Janet would smile and tell Stanley what a great husband he was.

Within a year, they started a family. Stanley wanted a son to help with the farm. But Janet had complications after giving birth to Kate and Suzy, and could no longer bear children. After the twins came home from the hospital, sleep was scarce, meals weren't always cooked, and the couple no longer made time for walks and talks. So Stanley worked harder, increasing his herd, and he purchased more land to harvest more crops. Yet he would not hire a helping hand—he told himself that no one could do the job the way he would have wanted. And he would not let Janet help, saying her place was in the house, keeping it clean, cooking the meals, and raising the children. He stopped confiding in her. Soon all Stanley did was eat, sleep, work, go to church, and play dartball.

His hands shook a lot and some nights he didn't sleep at all. His big, strong frame turned narrow and gaunt. The hair on his head became scarce—it helped to emphasize the hazel eyes that used to be so placid.

Stanley just kept getting worse.

Later This Afternoon
The twins play in their room upstairs. Janet bakes white rocket brownies while chatting on the phone. Stanley holds his rifle between his legs as he drives his John Deere in the fields. He travels on the same path that Janet used to walk with him.

Suzy pretends to give Kate art lessons. Suzy likes drawing and acting, while Kate prefers math and numbers. Suzy, being fifteen minutes older and one inch taller, tries to dominate and protect her younger twin.

The girls imagine they are in school. They sit on the wooden floor with a bucket of broken crayons between them. Mrs. Beasley and Drowsy sit in fake desks. Suzy draws black flowers with brown and red leaves. She says she is making clothes for Ken and Barbie. They talk to their dolls, saying they can't wait for summer vacation to be over.

Then bang-bang, gun shots fire. The girls look at one another. Downstairs Janet hangs up the phone. An odor, stronger than the manure smell, seeps into the home's windows.

Janet runs to the door. Her cooking buzzer rings and she runs back to the oven to take out the brownies. She can't smell them because the stench from outside takes over. She runs back to the door.

Suzy looks out the window and opens it. Kate crawls under the covers with her cow slippers on.

"What are your doing letting that smell in here?" Kate asks.

Suzy puts her face up to the open window and takes a deep breath. "I love it. It reminds me of Grandma's."

Kate thinks. Suzy walks to the bed. They recite the Lord's Prayer, taking long breaths, inhaling the scent.

Stanley stops the tractor in front of the white rocks. He runs to the house, stepping in old syrup. He pulls on the door handle and it wobbles. The twins run to their door and listen.

"Finally shot the skunks. Every one of em. Got em all. The whole family. Every one. Got em all," he says. "Got em out there in the field. Every one of em. Got em all." He wipes his rifle with his red handkerchief, then puts the gun into the cabinet and locks the door. "I got em all." Stanley paces, his boots sticking to the floor.

Janet follows him, taking small, apprehensive steps. She rubs her sweaty palms on her blue-checkered apron.

Sunday, July 4th

Stanley drives his family to church in his '97 Dodge Intrepid. He grasps the steering wheel with both of his shaky hands. He shifts his body in his seat and stares straight ahead, his eyes fixed on the bumpy road. The car needs new shocks, so he slows down each time he anticipates a pothole, which is something he's gotten used to. Puddles make spots on the blue car. Stanley hasn't slept much, and has eaten very little over the past week. This morning at breakfast, while staring at his eggs, he told his family he loved them.

Janet rides in the front seat and hums in her soprano voice songs that she has been recently singing with her Sweet Adelines group. She looks out the window and notices how green the fields have become since the recent rainfall.

The twins sit silently in the back seat, smelling Stanley's Old Spice. Suzy wants to hum along with her mother, but is too afraid. Instead she stares at her fingers and pretends to play the piano. Kate examines the white dots on her red pants and pretends there are lines connecting them.

The twins still wished Stanley were dead.

At church, the family sits in a white pew. They are afraid they smell like skunks. Like every Sunday, the girls sit between their parents, Stanley by the aisle, Suzy next to her father. Janet sits by Mrs. Meyer, the girls' former first-grade teacher, who offers Janet a hymnal. The Schukers bow their heads to pray, and while the organist plays a familiar melody, they wait for the service to begin. Stanley hits his fists on his knees while Mrs. Meyer stares. Janet looks at Mrs. Meyer's red lipstick and smiles while Suzy shifts closer to her sister. Stanley rests his elbows on his knees and buries his head in his hands. Suzy and Kate look at one another, while Janet silently hums the tune in her head and looks at the figure of Jesus that stands behind the pulpit. She thinks he looks so meek and kind.

In his white robe, Pastor George steps onto the pulpit and greets his congregation, which today is nearly two hundred. As he smiles and raises his hand to make the sign of the cross, Stanley yells, "God help me now!"

Pastor George drops his hands, forgetting his routine. He looks in Stanley's direction. The congregation stares in wonder. Suzy moves even closer to her sister.

The Hospital

Stanley lies in a hospital bed of the psychiatric unit while Janet holds his hand. Her bloodshot eyes mask their usual gray color. Stanley sleeps soundlessly in peace.

The girls stare out the window wishing they could be at the Fourth of July celebration, watching the parade, eating hot dogs, and playing in the playground with their friends. The hospital smell nauseates them. Suzy watches the cars that shuffle in the street below. Kate does the same.

"How about angel food cake tonight?" Janet asks.

The girls look at Janet, shrug their shoulders, look out the window again.

A nurse enters the room to take Stanley's vital signs, but he doesn't wake up. "He just needs his sleep," she says. "That stuff really knocked him out." Janet and the girls look at her, but say nothing, so the nurse quickly exits.

Bangs from illegal fireworks sound from outside. The sun shines.

Stanley grumbles in his sleep. The three look up at him. "Why is he so high up?" Suzy asks.

"Just because," Janet says.

Stanley's bed is raised to the highest level. A white sheet covers him, leaving his head and feet exposed. An overhead light shines on his face, making his skin glow. Then Stanley takes smooth, even breaths, his rhythm like a song.

"It's time we talk to God," Janet says. She caresses Stanley's rough fingers.

Kate, Suzy, and Janet gather round the bed. They bow their heads, fold their hands, then close their eyes and pray.

Hay

Two weeks later Janet drives Stanley home. She glides over potholes, making the car soar. Stanley unrolls his window and feels the warm breeze on his cheeks. The wind fills the car's interior, lunging into the back seat, where Kate and Suzy sit. Their hair flies.

The car crunches into the driveway. Janet opens Stanley's door. Stanley gets out and walks up the walkway, shuffling his feet. Janet puts her hand on his shoulder. The girls follow, taking miniature steps.

The air conditioning makes the house cold. Stanley walks through the door, scanning his surroundings. He enters the living room, and sits on the long cushioned sofa. Kate and Suzy rest in a matching chair, sharing it, sitting so close, they look like they're attached. They stare at Stanley.

In the kitchen, Janet makes hot chocolate.

Janet brings the drinks into the room on a green tray that is covered with a pattern of orange and red flowers. Steam rises from the cups.

Stanley stares at the TV screen. Tears well from his blank hazel eyes. Janet looks at him, then at the girls.

"Go upstairs for a little while," she says. The girls get up and start toward the stairs.

"No, wait," Stanley says. They turn back, looking at him. He pauses for a moment, then buries his head in his hands, sobbing.

"Go on, girls," Janet says.

The twins nod, then aim for the stairs. When they get to the landing they run, chasing each other to the top. Suzy wins. Kate shuts the door. They take off their shoes, then plop on the bed, staring at the ceiling. Kate puts on her slippers.

"Let's draw," she says.

"OK," Suzy agrees. They get out their crayons and make pictures, using an array of colors: blue, purple, yellow, and orange. They look at one another and pretend to smile, then go about their business.

Janet sets the tray on the table. She gives Stanley his cocoa. She brushes his wet cheeks with her soft hands. Then she sits next to him and puts her palms around her cup. It warms her. Stanley looks at his wife, admiring her. He blows on his drink, feeling its heat as the steam rises to his face.

From outside, a faint breeze filters in. It smells like fresh hay.

SHOT GIRLS

When Dot and Rache turned twenty-one, they thought they were invincible. They'd thought that way before, but somehow being twenty-one gave them an edge, as if it were some feat like running a marathon or hiking barefoot across the world. They were twins. They didn't dress the same, but they didn't try to look different, either. Dot's hair was always longer because it grew so fast. They shared a wardrobe, which they kept in one big walk-in closet, with outfits in sizes three and four, and forty pairs of shoes lined neatly on the carpet. They were still in college, and after their birthday they'd gotten jobs at a dance club called "The Heap." Dot was the "shot girl," and Rache was a bartender, although she wanted to be the shot girl too, but Dot got the job because she could sell a little more with the way she sometimes flaunted, though she wasn't proud of it. It was just the way she was. Rache was more reserved, but wanted to be like Dot. Sometimes, they envied one another. At the bar, guys would ask about them being twins, and Rache was stuck behind the bar, while the guys followed Dot on her rounds, going from table to table carrying racks of test tubes filled with drinks with sexy names—Blow Jobs, Screaming Orgasms, Watermelon Screws. Since the shot girl could wear what she wanted, Dot wore short skirts and skimpy tops. When it got late, she carried the tray above her head, getting fondled along the way, which came with the job. Sometimes she wished she were the bartender, just so she wouldn't always feel invaded, and she pictured herself with Rache's job, using the counter as her barrier, her Great Wall.

One day they walked to a tattoo shop by their apartment. The smell of the place reminded Dot of laundry detergent, and it made Rache think of the freshener in their mother's blue Toyota. They wanted identical tattoos, so Rache told that to the tattoo artist, the guy with his name, Frank, tattooed on his cheek.

He looked at them with their same blue eyes and thin dark hair, but he didn't say anything about it because he was too anxious to show them his tattoos. He took off his shirt, exposing the wispy vines and circles that wound around his chest and biceps, and a big red dragon that was spread across his middle. "It's horimono," he said. "Japanese tattoo art."

"We don't want to go that far," Rache said.

Dot sneezed and Rache said, "Bless you."

Since tattoos seemed so mainstream to them, they wanted something different and unique, yet something that would make them more alike, so they chose the Japanese character for friendship.

Afterwards they went home and freshened up before they had to go to work, feeling proud of what they'd done. Dot closed the blinds, looking down at the passing headlights, wishing she had enough money saved for her own car, and Rache flipped the TV to CNN, to a broadcast about Diana's death which wasn't new. People were crying on the screen, and Rache wondered what was wrong with them. Dot went to the end of the hallway to look in the full-length mirror, straightening it before unzipping her jeans so she could see her new tattoo. While she removed the gauze, Rache asked what she was doing, then went to see her tattoo in the mirror, too. They stood hip-to-hip, matching up their tattoos as if they were coded birthmarks. They compared their new tattoos, and each thought the other's looked better.

"Yours is darker," Rache said.

"I think it's inflamed," Dot said, touching it.

"I'm really glad we did this," Rache said.

"Me too," Dot said, putting her arm over Rache's shoulder.

They stood there for a while, looking at their reflections in the mirror, telling each other they made a perfect team.

That night, before going to work, they went to see their grandfather, who had had a stroke a month before. The left side of his face hung lower than the right, and he slurred his speech a bit. He'd lost weight, and stayed in bed a lot, although when Rache and Dot came to visit him, his face lit up and he tried to look like he was healthy. Since the stroke, he'd been staying with their mother, who worked as a medical assistant, and lived in a small brick ranch, where Dot and Rache had lived until their last birthday.

They walked in without knocking. Their mother was sitting in a chair beside the table, reading last week's Sunday comics, sipping on a cup of coffee, still wearing her blue scrubs.

"There's a fresh pot if you want some," she said, looking up. Then she went back to reading and the girls sat across from each other at the table, trying not to lean back on the chairs since their tattoo sites were stinging. They'd decided they weren't going to tell their mother about what they'd done that day.

"Grandpa still alive?" Rache said.

Their mother looked up quickly, saying, "Jesus, Rache, don't be saying things like that."

"I'm kidding," Rache said.

"How is he?" Dot said.

"You could stay with him every now and then. I can't afford the help."

"We're in college, Mom," Rache said.

"We could come between a couple classes," Dot said.

"We're all he's got," their mother said, curling up the corners of her paper.

Rache and Dot went into his room, where he was lying in the bed, clicking the remote, switching the show to *Lawrence Welk*. "Your grandma liked this guy," he said.

He was in his king-size, which the twins' mother had moved over in a U-Haul, with all his other stuff. Now he had the twins' old room, traces of them still left behind, the picture of them in their cheerleading uniforms, extending their arms to make a crooked W for the West Side Wolverines. The Boys 2 Men poster was taped up behind the bed, and a Brad Pitt centerfold was tacked to one side of the door. The TV was on the white dresser that they'd used since they were babies, that had held their small pink socks and training pants and frilly Sunday dresses, although recently it held their pastel bras and skimpy shorts and bright bikinis.

They sat on either side of him, and he smiled, the left half of his thin lips slightly paralyzed, which made his smile crooked. "How are my twin girls?" he said, slower than he used to, yet there was vigor in his voice, and it was as clear as an adolescent's whistle.

He put his arms around them as they crawled in like they did when they were younger and stayed with him, when they'd wake up early in the morning, smelling the coffee, scrambled eggs, and bacon that their grandmother had made, and they'd get under his sheets and rouse him, staring closely at his face, at the sleep still in his eyes, at the curl at the corner of his lips that made him look like he was smiling, which made them wonder what he had been dreaming. He was always warm under the covers, and as they woke him and he spoke, they could smell the newness of his breath, that was sort of sweet, and they watched the wrinkles forming under his green eyes as he smiled and welcomed them in his arms, into his waking world.

Now they still loved to cuddle under his soft covers, feeling the warmth of his aging body, and they felt like they were ten again, their grandmother scurrying in the kitchen, banging pots and pans, and right now, as he watched *Lawrence Welk*, Dot thought she remembered the melody that the band was playing, and not just that but some tender moment, although she couldn't recall exactly what it was. It was familiar to Rache too, but to her, everything about the show brought the same reaction, and she didn't cherish the memory quite like Dot, who had more affection for her grandfather.

They talked to their grandfather for a while longer, telling him about their jobs, about their school, explaining to him they still had to find a major. He didn't understand since he hadn't even graduated high school.

At the bar, Rache made the shots, and Dot wasn't on till nine, so she sat there smoking cigarettes. Rache looked at her sister, envying her perfect body, although Rache's was identical to Dot's, except she had longer arms, and she had on a pair of jeans and a sweatshirt that said "The Heap" in crooked golden letters. Dot shivered, and asked Rache if she could have a cup of coffee.

"Wear something for a change," Rache said, pouring the French Roast, then going back to funneling Baileys into narrow tubes.

"Have you ever seen a shot girl with long sleeves?" Dot said, flicking her lighter off and on. "I'm supposed to show my skin. It's my job."

"You can always bartend."

Dot lit a cigarette. "Maybe I'll call Frank."

"You're not afraid of anything."

"Nu-uh," Dot said.

"I wish I was the shot girl," Rache said, putting the whipped cream inside the silver compact fridge.

"No, you don't," Dot said. "You don't want this slutty job."

Later the place got packed, and Rache ran around behind the counter, spilling drinks over her long sleeves. Dot got burned in the face with a slender cigarette that a tall thin woman waved around, and then a big-necked guy in a Giants' sweatshirt grabbed Dot's ass. Dot pretended that she liked it, and asked him, "What's up, soldier? You want a body shot? I have a new tattoo."

He asked her where it was and she said, "In my panties," then he dropped a hundred in her glass and told her she could show it to him later.

At shut down, Rache had her sleeves up, wiping up the counters with a soppy rag while Dot sat at the bar. "We should find new jobs," Rache said.

"Some guy dropped a hundred in my glass. He wants to see the new tattoo."

"No shit? Jesus," Rache said. She was jealous. "Keep that up, and you'll be rich."

"Maybe we can apply for scholarships," Dot said. "Or maybe Mom will help us."

"Think again," Rache said.

"I guess it isn't all that bad," Dot said.

"Yeah, you're right," Rache said, picking up a broken bottle from a sticky tray. "It can be sort of fun."

Outside, the hundred-dollar guy was leaning up against the brick, toeing pebbles with his boot.

"That's the guy," Dot said. "You can go ahead."

"You'll be OK?" Rache said.

"I'm good at this. I'm a sleaze, remember?"

When Rache got to the corner, Dot turned to the guy. "What's up?" she said.

"You want to see my truck?"

"Yeah, OK," Dot said. She knew she shouldn't be going to some guy's car alone this late at night, but he looked innocent enough, and she knew she was a tease, and then she thought about the hundred dollars, figuring she must owe him something.

After they got to his truck, she pulled up her skirt and slid her panties down an inch, as if she were showing her driver's license to the Walmart clerk while buying Camel Lights. "There it is," she said.

He lit a cigarette. "My wife left me last week. I'm real young, separated. I don't want a relationship, just sex." He had nothing else to lose.

Dot had heard all that before, "no relationship, just sex, no relationship, just sex," as if it were some recording she'd heard so many times, a scratch on her favorite jazz CD, that kept replaying in her sleep, and she'd gotten used to it, knew when it was coming and didn't even think to fix it. Now she felt obligated.

Dot looked at the moving shadows that the flailing branches made. The streetlights shone past them, through the tinted windows of the truck. He kept looking out the window, then at her, then down at the floor, and Dot thought he was going to cry. She thought he needed cheering up, so she leaned over and unzip-ped his pants. When she was done, he took her home.

Rache was sitting on the sofa, watching a rerun of *Three's Company*, picking peanut chunks out of a jar of Skippy with a fork. She had been worrying about her sister, and feeling lonely and left out, when Dot walked in, dropping her purse and keys on the table by the door.

"How was the guy?" Rache said. The air conditioner hummed, sending a blast of cold across the room.

"Just like all the others," Dot said. "Don't worry. You didn't miss anything exciting."

The next night, he came back. He waited afterwards, leaning against the building, playing with a stick. Rache and Dot walked out together, and Rache leaned in toward Dot, telling her to ask if he had friends to set her up with.

When Rache walked away, Dot went up to him. The moon was full and bright, shining on his curly hair.

In the car, he said she didn't look old enough to be working at a bar, and she said he didn't care how old she was, and he admitted that was true. He said he felt sort of revengeful towards his wife, that the younger Dot was the better. He laughed to himself a little bit, then leaned over, kissing her. They took off all their clothes. His skin was hairless, smooth, like a sports car that had just been shined with Turtle Wax. After everything was over, Dot said, "I'm eighteen," pulling down her skirt and putting on her panties.

He rolled down the window and lit a cigarette. She watched him blow smoke out the narrow shallow gap. She looked at him, noticing his satisfaction.

When Dot got home, Rache was waiting, worried, anxious, just like always, and she asked Dot how it went, and Dot said it was great, that Doug was a super guy, and that they'd had sex in the parking lot.

"Oh," Rache said. "Really?"

Rache and Dot rummaged through the kitchen at their mother's, trying to find the chocolate cookies. "Shit," Dot said, looking into the black and white cow jar. "I bet Mom's boyfriend ate them all."

They made sandwiches with white bread, Miracle Whip, and fresh tomatoes from their mother's garden, and they left their knives sitting in the sink, then went to see their grandfather, who was lying in his bed. He was sleeping, and the TV was still on. It was MTV. They sat on the floor next to their dresser, close to one another, their backs leaning up against the wall. "He's not going to make it, is he?" Rache said.

His chest rose and fell and as he exhaled, his breath escaped through the gap in his front teeth, making a small whistle. It reminded Dot of a toy Santa they had when they were younger that blew in his sleep. "Looks like Santa," Dot said.

"I'm serious," Rache said. She was almost crying.

"He's only eighty-one," Dot said. "Grandpa Brunner died at 102."

They sat there, eating their sandwiches, then wiping off their lips with their paper towels, and they decided to let him sleep, so they left him a note, telling him how much they loved him.

For a couple weeks Doug waited for Dot, and she started staying at his motel room. He teased her, saying she was cheap, since she did anything he asked. She wanted him to be her boyfriend, yet she was content with having sex, figuring soon enough he'd divorce his wife, and realize how good she was to him. Rache felt left out, and she resented her sister for always putting her guys first. When Rache *did* see Dot, she asked if Doug had a friend for Rache to possibly go out with, but Dot said she could do much better.

One morning after Doug had brought Dot home, Rache and Dot sat on the checkered sofa at their apartment holding bowls of Raisin Bran, smelling the brewing coffee that had started automatically.

"So what if his friends aren't decent," Rache said, stirring her spoon, mixing up the sugar, scooping out a clump of raisins. "You always get the fun."

"I'm a slut," Dot said. "You don't want to be like me. It can be fun at first, but after a while, all you are is cheap. You can lose control."

"Well, I want some fun. I've only been with Roger, and that was only high school. How many guys have you been with? Twenty-something, right?"

"I lost count," Dot said. She got up and went into the kitchen, almost tripping over a stack of books. She set her bowl on the Formica, and she poured two cups of coffee, adding cream and sugar to Rache's purple cup.

A few nights later, after the bar was closed, Rache and Dot put on their leather jackets and stepped out, seeing Doug leaning up against the building in the alley.

"It's set," he said. "I have a friend for Rache."

"Not a loser, huh?" Dot said, reaching in her purse and pulling out her pack of smokes.

"Dot, stop it," Rache said, nudging her.

"She'll like him enough," he said.

Dot lit her cigarette. He said, "Come with me." After they walked to his truck, Rache slid in the tiny seat in back, anxious and excited, and Dot got in the front.

As he drove, Dot looked out the window, at the glowing lights, at the letters on the billboards, at the cars that they passed by.

"She's sexy," he said to Dot. "Just like you."

"Be nice to her," Dot said. "She's not a whore."

"I still want some action," Rache said, leaning forward. She was smiling, bright-eyed. She grabbed Dot's cigarette and took a drag.

"Don't worry," he said, "You'll get your share."

He drove to the Days Inn and stopped the truck. His room looked the same as always, shoes scattered on the floor, Ruffles bags and beer cans sitting on the table, and the TV was still on. He grabbed the ice bucket and said he'd be back, and then he left the room.

"I can't wait," Rache said, going to the mirror and touching up her eye shadow.

"Jesus," Dot said. "It's nothing special. You can get sex anywhere." She sat on the bed and Rache sat on a chair beside the table, toying with an empty beer can.

When Doug came back, he put ice in plastic cups and opened a Coke and poured it before adding shots of Jack. "My friend is coming in a minute," he said, giving Dot a drink, then Rache.

Dot took a sip right away, then slammed the rest, and Rache sipped slowly, saying she didn't want to be drunk when she met his friend. Doug opened a nightstand drawer and took out a joint and lit it, then sucked on it and handed it to Dot.

"Where you from?" Rache said.

"Nowhere special," he said.

"He's separated," Dot said, sucking in the joint.

"Yeah, I'm married," he said. "Dot takes care of me." He laughed.

"Like a Virgin" was playing on MTV. It was some Madonna marathon, and Dot started dancing on the mattress, moving in sync with the music, undoing the top button of her shirt, sliding a hand up and down her curves, balling up her other hand, putting it to her lips as if it were a mike. Doug told her she was crazy.

Rache sucked on the joint, then got on the bed and moved in front of Doug as if she were a stripper. "Where's my tip?" she said.

Another song came on and Rache poured herself more Jack. Dot felt dizzy and got down, leaning into Doug as he spun her around. "Hey," she said. "You spike these drinks, or what?"

He laughed and then she laughed and then they started kissing.

"Hey," Rache said. "When's my guy getting here?"

"Pretty soon," he said.

Dot plopped down on the bed. She felt funny, like things were fuzzy and she figured it was the joint, and she thought it worked rather quickly compared to the other stuff she'd done. It all belonged to Doug.

Rache was getting drunk. She took another hit, then laughed, and she grabbed Doug, dancing close to him.

Dot tried to get up, but she could barely move, so she lay back on the bed. She felt paralyzed. Then everything was black.

Doug's friend finally arrived, and Rache danced between the guys like a sandwich. She said she wanted to have a little fun. They talked to each other and to her, calling her a piece of trash, and Rache, said "Yeah, I am. Come and get me, hotshot." They kissed her, took off her clothes and she got on the bed and danced around, feeling like an exotic dancer, holding a beer in her right hand, raising it to the beat of the song on MTV.

Dot woke up first. She didn't know how long she'd been asleep. Could've been seconds, minutes, hours. It almost seemed like days. The place reeked of sweat and cigarettes and booze. She noticed her shirt was unbuttoned all the way, her skirt hiked up past her thighs. She pulled on her skirt's hem and as she buttoned her pearl buttons, she looked over on the floor, and saw Doug sleeping, and Rache lying next to him, naked, her hands tied behind her back, and a thick gold rope around her neck. On the second bed was a guy sleeping on his back, one leg hanging, his left toe touching the red carpet. He was snoring, but just so slightly that if she hadn't seen him, she probably wouldn't have noticed because of the racket coming from the air conditioner. His hair was long and stringy and his chest was hairless just like Doug's.

When Rache finally woke up, she could barely open her eyes. Her whole body hurt, and she didn't know where she was until she saw her sister, and then things started coming back to her. Dot untied her. "What happened here?"

"Holy hell," Rache said.

"Jesus," Dot said.

Dot helped Rache get dressed, lifting her shirt over her head, pulling up her jeans, then they sat around the table, on the plaid cushions of the wooden chairs. The morning light shone through the thick green curtains that were held together with shiny metal rods, and the TV was still on, its volume low, and there was some program on CNN, a pulled-together lady with bright lipstick.

The whole place smelled and looked like sex, like a porno movie that had gone on too long, gotten out of hand, the director and producer and the crew joining in even after the camera had gone off. Polaroids sat on the dirty table, snippets of ash floating all around them. In some of the photos, Dot was lying naked on the bed, her arms and legs sprawled out, Doug lying next to her, his hands between her thighs. In the other photos, Rache was naked, lying with her hands tied, and Doug's friend was on top of her, his back to the camera, his head turned with a half-grin on his face. Another was of Rache on her knees, Doug's jeans down past his hips, her legs and hands tied with that golden rope. Her bunched eyebrows and widened mouth that took him in made her look like she was screaming. Dot sifted through the pictures, tossed them across to Rache. "Jesus," Dot said. "We need to call the cops."

Rache shoved the pictures in her purse. "No way." She started a cigarette. "Some friends you have," she said.

"I'm a slut," Dot said. "We all know that."

Dot picked up Doug's Levi's from the floor and rummaged through his pockets. She took his wallet, cigarettes and keys. Then she found the other guy's gray shorts by his feet and felt his pockets, but all of them were empty.

"Over there," Rache said, pointing to the nightstand that was filled with empty cups, and wet from melted ice cubes.

Dot picked up his wallet, letting the water drip. She looked at his driver's license. "His name is Len," she said. "What a stupid name. Guy's only twenty-one."

"You're not going to steal it, are you?"

"Like they didn't steal from you?"

"I said I was fine," Rache said.

Dot got the Jack, went for the beer, then grabbed the guys' clothes and put them in the bathtub and soaked everything with booze. She opened the dresser drawers and dumped the catsup and the mustard that she'd gotten from the fridge on all of Doug's belongings. She hiked up her skirt and pulled down her panties and urinated on the bed where Len was sleeping. She wiped her crotch with a faded pillowcase that looked a shade of yellow.

"You're such a freak," Rache said.

"Serves him right," Dot said.

Rache turned off the TV, and Dot stuffed all the wallets and keys inside her purse. She messed up the sheets, and wrote on a piece of Days Inn paper, "This isn't over," and left it on the bed.

"I'm telling you," Rache said. "It wasn't all that bad."

They opened up the door, and the new sunlight was dim, but it made their eyes hurt. Rache and Dot looked back, then sat on the lawn next to the pool and Rache leaned against a tree. They just sat there for a while, staring at the uneven rays reflecting off the water, at the dirty edges of the pool, at the blades of grass drifting off in numerous directions. "I guess we better go," Dot said. And then they got up, and walked arm-in-arm for a couple blocks, and they knew they were close to home, but too far to walk in the state they were both in. So they walked to an Exxon station and Dot called a cab, and they waited on the curb in silence, just sitting feeling the warm sunrise, watching cars pass by, ones driven by people who looked as if they were on their way to work.

"We have to call the cops," Dot said.

"No," Rache said. "No cops. What's the difference between Doug fucking me and fucking you? Same with the other guy? You would have done it too."

"I asked for sex with Doug," Dot said.

"So did I," Rache said.

"Not like that," Dot said.

Rache told her she was fine, that everything was fine.

They got tired of waiting for the cab, so they got up and strolled along the sidewalk. Trash lay on the curb, McDonald's bags, and broken beer cans, a pack of crumpled cigarettes. A loud truck zoomed by and the driver honked its horn. The sun was hot, but the air was still a little chilly. Small clouds wandered overhead.

They walked along the edge of the Bay, streetlights glowing down, sunrise peeking up. Birds were singing over the drum of the distant train that came through town at the same time every morning. Dot took the wallets from her purse and counted all the money, about a hundred dollars, and she gave Rache half. Dot handed Len's wallet to Rache and took Doug's credit cards and tossed them in the water, one by one, but all they did was float. Dot looked at the pictures in Doug's wallet, one of him and his pretty brunette wife, and she crumpled it and tossed it overhand just like a baseball.

"Look at this," Rache said. She handed Dot a picture of a young girl in a purple swimsuit sitting on a swing. There were four snapshots, each with different poses. "That's odd," Rache said. She put the pictures in her purse, and then removed the photos from last night and filtered through them, one by one.

"I wonder if he'll come back," Rache said.

"He never will," Dot said, tossing Doug's wallet in the water, watching it splash before it sunk.

"He's going to need his wallet," Rache said. She studied the picture of her on her knees in front of Doug. She handed it to Dot.

Dot stared at it, looking at Rache's face. Dot almost started crying. She took Rache's pictures and threw them in the water. She watched them as they turned with the small wind that made the water stir.

"I guess that was pretty awful," Rache said.

"Are you kidding? It was horrible. A nightmare," Dot said. "Let's not do that again."

She remembered how they used to dare each other to jump into the Bay, how they'd feed the seagulls tiny breadcrumbs, letting the birds get so close they pecked the girls' bare feet. Now Dot stared at the falling moon's reflection on the water, and she thought she saw a figure, like a girl, floating on the bay, moving in a quiet motion with the gentle chilling waves. It was Rache, it was just the way she pictured things ending up, Rache floating in the Bay, shining in the watery light.

They sat on a bench and rested, watching a small boat slither by, sending a slight wave in the water. A bird landed on a wooden stump, perching its beak upward, turning its petite head at a slender angle. Then it spread its wings and flew away.

"I know why Grandpa loves you more," Rache said. "You've always been the brave one."

"That's not true," Dot said. She heard a splash coming from the water, a fish jumping like the jack-in-the-box they had when they were kids. "Remember that time we went fishing in the lake? And you and Grandpa did the breaststroke? Racing across while I stayed in the boat? I was scared to death. And then you won, so he bought you extra ice cream. I was so upset. I hated going fishing." She looked at her sister. The air was getting hot.

Rache put her arm around Dot, feeling her lean arms, feeling the strength in all their smallness. She said, "We are *so* alike."

YOU WERE ONE

It wasn't your fault the door wouldn't lock. It wasn't your fault you loved your dogs so much you hugged them where they lived in the barn, then you got spanked because of bringing in the dog hair. It wasn't your fault you turned purple—bruised—because your dad got mad, because you didn't peel an orange right. It wasn't your fault you let in your dad when your mother begged you not to. It wasn't your fault he kept calling you a screw-up. You were one and two and three and four and five and six, seven, eight and nine and ten and eleven and twelve and thirteen. How was it your fault, on that one day, sitting next to him in church, your dad shouted out for his Lord God to save him? It wasn't your fault that the pastor and the congregation halted, with their eyes on you.

Wasn't it nice, some days, when you could run out to the field? Circling and spinning? Looking up? Just putting your arms out?

MY LITTLE FEET

I stand high and try to touch the nose of a sculpture named after a victor. I imagine him alive, before my time, holding his tablet, with his legs crossed. His declarations that brought peace to my country.

I touch his shoe, noticing a dark spot.

After he was shot, his procession travelled through this city. I imagine stepping where he may have stepped.

I turn to look at a tiny pond, with foliage sprouting out of it.

I take an exodus and run back home to carve my fairytale pumpkin for a party that starts at midnight.

BIG BIRD

Kel's husband died in a car crash in his girlfriend's blue Miata, leaving Kel and their four-year-old son Sam in North Dakota. Kel had to pay the bills he left behind, so even though she was a cop full time, she got a part-time job at a bar called Boogie Nights. She'd leave Samuel in the break room while she worked, then make her rounds with the men she waited on, meeting them after the bar was closed-up for the night, with Sam sleeping in the back seat of the car, his body twisted, limbs like a doll's, head propped up on Big Bird.

This night, at her place, after Kel got off the phone with Harlow, a cop she worked with who had been the best man at her wedding, she gave Samuel liquid Tylenol before she left for work, since he wasn't feeling well. "No medicine!" he screamed. Kel spooned the syrup in his mouth, and it spilled across his face, so she wiped it with a napkin.

"I don't want to go," he said.

"I don't either," she said.

At work, she set Samuel up in back, unfolding the cot and rolling out his sleeping bag. He cried, holding out his arms. "I'll buy you a special treat if you're good tonight," she said.

The bar got packed and Kel strutted around, looking at people's cups to see how full they were. A guy she'd seen before, Dave, leaned into a blonde girl with a tight pink shirt that showed her cleavage. He cocked up his chin, said to Kel, "Get us two shots, will you? Goldschlager if you have it."

When she returned, the blonde was gone. Kel set the drinks down, and he handed her a fifty, telling her to keep the change. He looked like he was from a movie or a music video, with dark shiny hair and smooth skin and perfect teeth. Kel stared at him. She sat in the blonde woman's chair. "You some TV guy?" she said.

"Just plain Dave," he said, reaching for her hand.

She asked for his number, and he wrote it on a napkin. Then the blonde came back, and Kel tucked his number in her pocket and went back to work.

An hour later, the bar was cooling down so Kel punched out. She watched Samuel sleeping on the cot, in his brown pajamas, hugging his bird pillow. She didn't want to disturb him. She put her tip money in her purse, and washed her hands, then went out to the bar and ordered rum and Coke, paying with her tips. Dave was at his table, and the blonde was gone. Kel sat next to him and asked him where his friend went. "Ditched me," he said. "Found some other guy."

"Women are like that," she said.

He grinned at her and ordered shots of Goldschlager from one of the waitresses who was still working. Kel slammed hers, hoping the alcohol would calm her. Dave said he was an inventor, telling her the things he had invented, and about what he had to do to get a patent. She told him cop stories she made up, amusing herself with the situations she invented, thinking of how stupid he was to actually believe her. She did a few more shots, and started working on Dave's neck.

"We can go to my place," he said.

"I have to get my Sam," she said.

She got Samuel, who was sleeping.

They went out to her car and she gave Dave her keys. When they got to Dave's apartment, he helped Kel get Samuel up the stairs.

Inside, papers were everywhere, ashtrays spilling on the coffee tables, crushed beer cans on the dirty carpet. The nation's anthem blared from the TV, and a Dominos box sat on the leather sofa. Dave turned the TV off, and put the pizza box on the floor, and they lay Samuel on the sofa, covering him with a blanket. Kel put her purse by Samuel's feet.

In Dave's room, he shoved his piled clothes onto the floor, and started taking off his shirt. Kel lay on the bed, but he grabbed her hand and sat her up. She started laughing. "Taking advantage of me, are you?"

"You want me to?" he said, moving his hands across her back.

"Worse things have happened," she said. The room was spinning.

"You're a tease," he said.

She looked at Dave's eyes, at the sweat falling from his brow, and she heard his gasps and quiet aahs. She went limp then. He never even kissed her.

Kel woke up and looked around the room. She threw the covers back and looked at her watch. It was eight a.m. She had to work for the police at nine. She sat up, and found her clothes under the sheets. Dave was sleeping on her shirt. She shoved him over.

She left the room, a guy in the hall wearing boxers passed her and he looked at her, smiling. She went to the living room, where Samuel was watching *Scooby Do*.

"We have to go," she said.

"Whose house is this?" he said. He took a bite of the Snickers he was holding.

"Just some guy's," she said. "Where'd you get that candy?"

"From a big man with drawings on his chest. He told me you were sleeping with his friend."

"Jesus," she said. "Let's go."

She got to the car, then noticed she didn't have her purse, so she told Samuel to stay right where he was. She'd already forgotten which apartment was Dave's, so she knocked on random doors, and when he opened his, he said, "What's the problem."

"I forgot my purse," she said.

She went in, spotting her bag on the sofa.

She drove a few blocks, then realized she was in a town she'd been to a few months ago with Harlow, where they'd gone skinny dipping.

Kel drove on the highway to Grand Forks. It was a forty-mile drive. She turned up the heat, but then she got too hot, so she cracked the window open. Samuel put his pillow over his face. The wind was strong, and Kel held the wheel steady. The view was flat and there were only fields and skies for miles.

When she got home, she took a shower and got dressed, then called the station, saying she'd be late again. She took Samuel to daycare, kissing him.

Now Kel was on cop duty. She drove out to the flight line, and she just sat there, smelling aircraft fumes, hearing the loud engines as they revved, and she smoked her cigarette, watching planes as they took off, vanishing like big metal souls ascending into heaven. Everything was flat, and the wind was strong, and there was nothing beyond the runways but one big piece of land. It looked like a painting.

Sometimes other cops lined up their cars, side by side, talking over the loud engines.

Today Harlow was talking about a girl he had the hots for. "She's something else," he said.

"She pretty?" another cop named Scout said.

"Geez, you guys," Kel said, dropping her smoke in a can. "Does that really matter?"

"She's kind of like you," Harlow said.

"I beg your pardon?" she said, looking at the mechanics crawling over the jets back up by the hangars.

Scout got a call on a domestic then flicked on his sirens and sped away. Harlow said, "You working at the club tonight?"

"You coming?" Kel said.

Before Kel worked that night at the bar, she went to see her grandmother, Violet, at the nursing home, where she'd been living since Kel's grandfather passed away ten years before. Violet was eighty.

Kel held Samuel's hand and they walked through the automatic doors, stepping through the lobby, where white-haired people watched the *Wheel of Fortune*, some laughing, some sleeping, and a tall obese man yelled out for a nurse, calling her his daughter. The place always smelled stale, but today it smelled like bleach. Samuel sucked on a Life Savers that Kel had given him, then he bit it into pieces. They walked down the hallway, and two old ladies in thin gray robes looked at them, tilting their white heads. One woman's head was shaking frantically, and Kel smiled at her.

In the room, Violet was on the bed, staring at the ceiling, her hands folded, and she was whispering something Kel didn't understand. Kel sat at the bedside, and Samuel went up to the bed and grabbed his great-grandmother's hand. "Nana," he said, and Violet turned her head, and a smile lit her wrinkled face. "Nice to see you," she said.

"Hi Grandma," Kel said. She got up from the chair and leaned over her grandmother and kissed her. "I didn't want to interrupt. You looked like you were praying."

"I pray all the time," Violet said, her voice small and quiet. She squeezed Kel's hand.

Samuel got up on the bed. He sat next to his great-grandmother, and he put his arm around her. He pointed to the TV that hung from the wall in front of the bed. "Barney on?" he said.

"Barney doesn't come to Grandma's house," Kel said. Samuel looked at Violet's face and started laughing. Violet laughed too. Kel walked up to the window and looked down. "Are you OK here?" she said. "I mean, are they treating you OK?"

"I'm fine," Violet said. "But the string beans are no good."

Violet's roommate entered. "Hi Ethel," Kel said, but the woman just walked past them.

On the way to the bar, Kel thought about her grandmother, wondering how she could be happy at a place like that. Her grandmother never seemed to mind it, and Kel thought about what it would be like if her grandmother lived with her. After Kel's grandfather died, Violet seemed so humble and reserved. When he was alive, he and Violet were always going places, traveling across the country, doing good things for underprivileged people. Kel was sixteen when he died. Now she was twenty-six. Kel remembered when her parents and her grandparents would get together for holidays and weekends, eating turkey, ham and stuffing, and the cornflake wreath with green food coloring and cherries splashed across it, how they'd sit around the player piano, watching the keys move up and down, how they'd sing along, all off tune and making up new words so they would rhyme. They all seemed so happy, like those TV programs where nothing seems it could go wrong, but then someone gets shot or gets killed by a drunk driver, only on TV not everybody dies. Her parents passed before she was a toddler. And now even Kel's husband passed away, something she feared the whole time that she'd known him, and even though he'd shoved her around way too much, she wished he were there, just so she could tell him she was lonely.

Kel had been daydreaming so hard, she sped by Boogie Nights, so she did a U-turn. When she got there, she gave Samuel his new LEGO's and opened the cot, and told him she'd be back to check on him when she wasn't busy.

She waited tables, the music boomed, and the place got smoky. Dave was with the blonde who'd ditched him. Then Harlow and Scout and other cops came in. Harlow said she had nice legs and she said thanks and looked at Dave, who was touching the blonde's bare knee with his thumb. On Harlow's way to the bathroom, he passed Kel at the bar. She leaned over. He put his arms around her.

She turned around and whispered in his ear, "Meet me after."

At closing, Dave held up the blonde, and Kel went in back, where Samuel was sleeping, and she handed him to Harlow. She gave him the keys to her Toyota. After clean-up, she ran to her car, since it was so cold. Harlow was waiting, heat blasted, radio on, leaning his seat back. Samuel was sitting in the driver's seat, turning the wheel.

She got in and told Samuel to get in back, then she started the car and backed out of the lot.

"You did good in there," Harlow said. "Seems like you own the place."

"I've got it down," she said. The car almost swerved into the ditch.

"Good for you," he said.

"You coming over?" Kel said.

"What about him?" Harlow said, nodding toward the back.

She said, "He really likes you."

"I'm hungry," Samuel said. "Can we go to that burnt pancake place?"

"We have food at home, Hun," Kel said. She looked at Samuel in the rearview. He was poking Big Bird in the eye.

After they got home, she made Pop Tarts for Samuel, and coffee for herself. Harlow sat at the table watching Samuel. "There's something wrong with this," he whispered to Kel.

"With what?" she said. She got up and poured more coffee and he stood behind her.

"Samuel going to work with you. Waking up at two a.m. Being hungry. He must miss his dad."

"Have a solution?"

"Jeff wouldn't like all this," Harlow said.

"Jeff is gone," she said. "You didn't think he was so great when I was getting black eyes."

Kel put Samuel to bed and when she came out, Harlow grabbed her hand. They'd known each other six years. She led him to her room, where the streetlight filtered through the blinds, making everything looked striped. He told her that he'd been talking about her that day in the car.

It was the first time they made love.

The next morning, after Harlow left, Kel thought about how good he'd been to her. Harlow was always there when her husband wasn't, when her husband was out late with his girlfriend, who Kel had known about, but never mentioned because she was afraid of getting beaten. Now she wasn't afraid of getting beaten, but she was afraid of falling in love. She decided to call Dave. She'd found the crumpled napkin in the kitchen drawer.

He came over on a Tuesday. They drank wine from Martini glasses, and Samuel drank Kool-Aid.

"What's your name again?" Samuel said to Dave.

"His name is Dave," Kel said.

Samuel asked if he was the guy she called a loser. Dave laughed.

"I'm an inventor," he said. "What you going to be when you grow up?"

"An architect," Samuel said.

"He likes art," Kel said. "And he loves all kinds of buildings."

After Samuel went to bed, Dave and Kel sat on the sofa, sipping the red wine he had brought over. He finally kissed her. His breath was sweet and strong and grapelike. The phone rang, and she let the answering machine pick up and it was Harlow, saying he just wanted to say hi.

"Who was that?" Dave asked.

She said, "One of my dead husband's friends."

Dave asked if he could take a shower, and although she thought it was a little strange, she said, "Sure," then showed him where the towels were, and asked him to wipe the shower with a cloth when he was done, then spray the panels with the Shower Clean. As he showered, she listened to Harlow's message, and she thought about calling him. Then Dave came out of the bathroom, towel wrapped around him, and she smelled her soap on him, and it made her feel sexy. She slid up from her chair and touched his chest and kissed him.

They started dating, although she told him she didn't want a boyfriend. He said he didn't want a girlfriend either. She knew she'd never love him. He was someone to spend time with. After a couple weeks, Dave said his friends weren't letting him stay with them anymore, since he couldn't pay the rent, and he told Kel he was waiting for a big check for a new invention, and he volunteered to babysit if she let him live with her. She thought of all the money she could save on daycare, and not having to hear Harlow telling her that her husband wouldn't be happy with the way she was living. So she said OK, and Dave brought his stuff over.

But after a few weeks, she'd meet guys at the bar and end up at some motel, or some apartment. When she got home, Dave would be upset, and she would remind him of their agreement. "No strings attached," she said. Dave told her that if she didn't straighten out, he'd call social services, that Samuel was better off with him. Sam always seemed to listen more to Dave, not complaining or crying like he sometimes had with Kel.

And she'd been avoiding Harlow. Even at work, she didn't talk to him, telling him she was too busy or too tired. She wanted to be alone, except when she was at the bar, where she could talk to people about things that didn't matter much, like what did they want to drink, or how were they going to pay, or could she clean their ashtrays. And then afterwards, when she was having sex with just some guy, she didn't really have to talk, but she could touch him and be near him in that way, which was good enough, better than making some attachment, where she would care too much, and this way it didn't matter what happened, because it was just one night, one hour, or one day. To Kel, it wasn't really life. It was just one episode followed by another. One clip on a film. Everything, an act.

Sometimes she would watch Samuel playing with his LEGOs, or talking to his Big Bird, and she saw her husband in his face, and she remembered how she'd thought she really loved him, and she felt so helpless. And the few times Samuel let her hold him and he seemed happy, Kel felt like she was doing something right, that maybe there was some hope, but she was scared when she felt things like that, because she'd felt that way before, and then it was gone in just an instant, like when her parents died, and her grandfather had that heart attack, and then, all that stuff with her husband. It was like a recurring tornado or a hurricane destroying someone's home after it had been rebuilt once, twice, three times, and the homes never got any stronger, but they just got weaker every time, more and more run down. And now, for Kel, feeling safe scared her because she knew nothing was for sure, that anything could just vanish any time, so she convinced herself that being scared was something she should be feeling *all* the time.

A month later, after an all-nighter, she went home and stopped the car, and she looked in the rearview and wiped her smudged mascara with a tissue. She put her hair in a barrette she'd found in her purse, trying to think of a new excuse so Dave wouldn't get upset. She'd used every excuse her husband had, and she'd almost become fond of him for that, thinking at least he'd taught her something. She parked in the drive, and on her way to the front door, she tripped on a hoe. All the blinds were shut. She checked all the rooms—Dave and Sam were gone. She checked the phone for messages. She found a note next to the phone. "We're fine," it said in loopy writing. She realized she was shaking, and thought maybe she should call someone, but she figured she didn't know that many people. She called Harlow. He wasn't home. Then she called Dave's old number, but the guy who answered didn't have a clue. Finally she called the police. Two guys she knew a little came out and took the report. They were friendly, and Kel was relieved that they didn't say, "I told you so," although she thought that was what they were probably thinking. They almost looked like twins, both with flattops, chewing wads of gum. They nodded a lot and frowned, looking sympathetic, putting their chubby hands on her shoulders.

Kel didn't do anything besides wait for the phone to ring.

People had been looking. There were search teams everywhere. Samuel's pictures had been plastered at every Laundromat, on postcards and the Net, on the news and radio, even at the grocery. She thought of the last time she'd seen Samuel, bouncing on a bean bag, his blond bangs flapping on his forehead. He'd seemed happy.

Harlow came over the first night, knocked on her screen door, stepped inside and held her, saying he was sorry. She gripped his collar, saying, "Where *is* he?"

"I'm sorry for you, Kel," Harlow said. He pulled her closer.

"I was wrong. I should have listened. You were right." She fell into him, crying on his pocket. He said he didn't want to break her heart any more than it was already broken.

They sat together on the sofa. She sobbed while Harlow sat there. After she was quiet, she moved next to him, leaning on his shoulder. He put his arm around her and told her not to worry.

Now it was days, and Kel called the cops again to get an update. Nothing, she sat up, drinking coffee, staring out the window. She grabbed her cell phone, and got in her car and drove. She didn't know where she was going. At the intersection, she turned right. A man walked across the road and she almost hit him. She thought she saw Samuel poking his head out of the bushes, the kind of thing she'd imagined ever since he had been gone, like every time she'd misplaced her keys, and then she'd find them in the weirdest places: under a Sunday paper, or by the kitchen sink, or in a shoe, or in Samuel's daycare bag.

It was almost dark. The sunset was falling on the trees in crooked patterns, and the air was cool, the wind just slight. She drove through all the flatness and the nothingness and when she stopped on a yellow light at an intersection she didn't know which way to turn. She heard a train wailing in the distance, and she looked in her rearview, and saw the lights of a small car stopping behind her. She decided to wait for the yellow to turn red, then wait for the green. She'd go on green. She'd go straight on the green light.

She drove to the nursing home.

Violet was staring up at the ceiling just like always, hands folded, praying, as if she already was in heaven, or if she was just waiting to be taken.

Kel sat on the vinyl chair, pale-faced, blank, as if she were a dummy. "Dave ran away with Samuel."

Violet turned her head. "I'm praying for him now."

Kel grabbed a tissue from Violet's table, folded it in squares, unfolded it, then folded it again. "It's all my fault."

Violet shook her head. She said, "I love you."

Kel looked up from the floor, up at her grandmother. Tears ran down Violet's face. The last time Kel saw her grandmother cry was at her parents' funeral. Kel grabbed Violet's hand. It felt like a dry strawberry, like the ones they used to pick together at the patch, their skin getting burned even though they always used protection. "Do you want to live with me?" Kel said.

After a while Violet said, "This has been my home for years." She said. "I could never live with you."

Kel sat there, staring at the window in the distance, at the dark. The streetlights flickered. "I better go," she said.

"Tell Samuel to be good," Violet said. She folded her hands again.

Kel closed her eyes, wondering what her grandmother was praying about, who she was praying to. Kel tried not to think too hard. Elderly people passed in the hallway, silently and calm, stepping deliberately, one foot after the other. They were not going anywhere. Kel watched her grandmother and thought about calling Harlow. She thought about her husband and the girl, that blue Miata. Then she thought of Samuel. She wondered if she could pray like Violet. So she tried that. She folded her hands like Violet. She told herself that if there wasn't a god to pray to, she'd just pray to the sky. She imagined that. She figured it was something.

ELEPHANT

Peel the damn potato, my grandma yelled from the kitchen to my grandpa, who sat at the sewing machine in his straw hat, embroidering bright patterns of zoo creatures onto my new church clothes.

Boom boom! went the fireworks.

Boom boom! went all the people's voices.

I went to my grandma's room and found her favorite lipstick. Put some on my lips and slipped it in my pocket.

I went outside and sat on the tire that hung from the biggest tree I'd known.

I moved my feet. I kicked.

Boom! Boom!

Boom! Boom! Boom!

WHAT MIGHT BE

When he plays his piano, his chords ring softly in the sunlight. His dog barks at who might be coming to the door. Later on, he records his music in his studio, that was once, before he owned it, a child's bedroom, balloons wallpapered on the walls, and then, there were cries and coos ringing all throughout that baby's bedroom. Now he strums his old acoustic, and this woman, who stands outside, waiting by the door, she only wants to listen.

She hears him playing, and the wind is a slight whisper. The dog is no longer barking, and this man has ceased playing his guitar and singing, from what she hears, so she puts her finger to the doorbell, and she remembers that this ringing is defective, so she knocks lightly on the wooden door, underneath its window, and she hears him say, "Come in," as she's often heard before.

She hears the dog approaching, hearing the eagerness throughout his panting.

After she arrives, you can hear them softly talking. If you are outside, you can't hear what they are saying. Maybe he is offering her a beer, or maybe he is telling her about an encounter with a stranger. If you are inside, you can hear him recalling events of his day, how he got up and practiced early in the morning, how his hands ached because he'd been pressing on his keys throughout the noon and evening, how his fingers bled from strumming his guitar. He might ask her how her day was, and it might take her a while to answer, because mostly, she just tries to listen. She really only wants to listen.

Sometimes they are laughing. And sometimes, you can hear the movie that is playing on his laptop. This is after all the talking. There is silence, mostly. There will be the movie playing, and they can hear the dialogue together, curled in his bedroom, under the warmth of his sheets and down, and they are so close, they can hear each other breathing.

Sometimes, when they are sitting on the porch, they can see the stars. One time, when she was coming over, she saw his shadow through the window. He was playing his piano, and she watched his long and slender arms. She found it elegant, eccentric. She only wanted to stand outside and watch the beauty of his movement. She closed her eyes, and wondered what he might be playing. She loved to imagine, for she'd heard him play before. But now, she was only seeing. She loved what her eyes said about what she'd heard before, what they left for her sound imagination.

She knocked on the wooden door, underneath the window. She sensed, and saw him coming, and she remembered then that it was him, as if, since yesterday, she had forgotten. He was tall and slim, and today he was wearing a T-shirt, plaid shorts, and a pair of white sneakers. His wire glasses sat snugly on his nose, and she knew, by the glowing look of him, that he was maybe working really hard, probably looking at his notes, his fingers synchronizing with the keys of his piano, and she saw something in him that she always wished she'd had, a talent for beautiful, extraordinary music.

She saw him smiling down at her, and then, again, she saw him, leaning in to her. He was offering her a kiss, so she closed her eyes, and she let her intuition lead her. There wasn't darkness as she kissed him. Then she opened up her eyes, seeing the man smiling, and she was smiling back at him, and then she looked down and saw the dog, big and black, and wagging, so accepting, as if she would never be a stranger, and she leaned over petting him, and she felt as if she belonged, as if she were a member of their household. She looked away for just an instant, and she saw a lot of things, like his stereo, his grand piano, sheets of music that were piled like a platform.

She looked back at him, and she wondered how he saw her.

He once told her, that, with her, he doesn't want anything romantic. He said he doesn't feel it. He said he didn't believe it. She remembers when he told her. She doesn't remember when it started. She heard nothing else. She always wanted to ignore it.

Steam rises from his kettle. His house smells like aftershave. And it smells like French Roast, or maybe cappuccino. It's a humid scent. It isn't quite the summer, although the weather teases them, telling them it could be.

The man doesn't smell anything right now, not that he can notice. He is practicing his music. He is playing his guitar, writing a new song, although he doesn't have the words, isn't thinking about lyrics. Right now, chords and notes and scores are all that matter. He might smell the burning of the kettle, after it is empty, and the burner gives off an eerie scent, but he won't notice right away, and when he does, it is not the scent that first alarms him.

When the woman arrives, she notices the remainder of the burning scent. She also notices the familiar scent, the one that always lingers, not knowing why it might remind her of some other place or time or maybe some ex-boyfriend. She doesn't know which one. Maybe it is bleach, or wood polish, or maybe window cleaner. She smells him when he leans over, into her, when he offers his embrace. She accepts it. She loves his naked scent.

She knows that he's been working because she notices a hint of sweat that reminds her of when they are together, sleeping, and she loves this part of him, this part that maybe only she, and none of his other lovers, might remember. She smells the dog as he comes between her and the man, separating them, as if he is their only toddler, begging for all of their attention. The dog smells like any other dog she can remember. She never really liked the scent of dogs, but now, there is something endearing in this scent, as if this is a small detail of this drawing, this picture of this home, this place, this life of this man who is her friend, who is blessed with gifts and intuition, this man who is her lover. She leans down, petting the dog behind his ears, and his body moves like a flimsy stick, and she smells his breath, and she breathes into him. "Pretty dog," she wants to say, but we are talking about smells here.

When she remembers what he said, about not wanting anything romantic, she is disappointed. Yet she is, maybe, unknowingly, relieved. This could mean that she will not be threatened, not be afraid that they will get too close, but this also means that he will be looking for another. He tells her that she is not the one. She does not believe that anyone has a one and only. Maybe she will never have to tell him all there is to know about her.

This night, when she arrives, she sees a reflection of him sitting, his arms outstretched, and she thinks, by what she is seeing, that he is inside, playing his piano. She wonders what he might be playing. As she is getting closer, she sees that he is outside, sitting on his swing, and the lights from the inside are glowing out at him, thus, showing his reflection. As she approaches, she sees that he is smoking. She sees the movement of his arm, his pointed elbow, and she imagines that he is inhaling. She sees the end, and yes, he is inhaling, the light is faintly glowing, getting brighter as it is expanding. It is burning. She sees the swing, then she is sitting next to him, and she is with him, swinging.

They are looking at a tree. The tree is planted in the front, and in reality, it is all that they are seeing. He says, "That tree looks like a hand," and she looks at it, at the trunk, and she sees that the trunk is like a wrist, and the branches are all fingers. She puts up her hand, looking at her fingers, that once played on her piano, looking at those fingers in all of their extensions. Yes, she says. She believes that he is right. She is in agreement. She says that it looks like the state where she is from. She reminds him that she is from Wisconsin.

She loves seeing all these things. There is beauty, hope. It gives her something to believe in.

This night, when she is in his bed, she wakes up crying. She cannot stop herself from crying. She can barely hear herself. She hears him ask her what is wrong. But she doesn't know. She says she doesn't have an answer. Later on, after she is quiet, she hears him breathing in his sleep.

She hears him, saying the next morning, telling her, that after the crying, she was talking in her sleep. She was speaking, shouting, reciting something, calling out in repetition. She hears him tell her she was almost singing, like she was talking to a devil, to a god, or maybe to somebody's ghost or to an angel. He says she was chanting. She says she doesn't know how she could do that. He says he's never heard anyone sing or speak that way before.

Sometimes, they go out for coffee. The texture of those wooden tables, they are smooth, and some of them are rough, depending on the perception of your fingers.

At the coffee shop, he tells her that he loves her. He is working on his laptop, and she has come to visit him between the teaching of her classes. She hears this man, telling her he loves her. But there are so many other things around, the clanging of the glasses, the people talking, ordering a drink or maybe two, a bagel, or a tuna salad. Some of them around the other tables are conversing, whispering small, or maybe some important talk with one another. Chairs behind her are being pushed aside, and she hears them as they rub against the hardwood floor.

This woman has no other lover. This woman has a roommate, and a cat, and a job teaching disadvantaged children. She once had a child herself. She once had a husband. But this is not that story. This is not the story of her husband or her child.

This is a story about seeing, smelling, hearing. This not a story about what this woman has forgotten, not a story about childhood.

This is a story about senses. This is a woman who has wanted. It is not about her brother nor her father, not about a man who might have raped her. This is not about what might have happened with her husband. This is a story of this woman's need, of her indulgence.

They go to the movies. They smell, they eat the popcorn. They see previews, the actors, the credits on the screen. They hear the people talking. They feel the salt of the popcorn on their fingers.

He believes in something. What he believes in she will never be a part of. She wants to believe in something beautiful and lasting. She listens to her senses. She is hearing, smelling, seeing. She is watchful, being.

The birds wake them in the morning. They squawk outside the bedroom window. The dog comes into the room, and barks along. They have not set the clock. She says she has to go. He looks at her and asks her to come over later on and listen to his music. She does not remind herself that she will never be the person who he dreams of. She already knows this. She is listening. She will go to work, and she will teach the children.

She reminds him that she loves him. She wants to hear his music. He smiles. She says she will be back. She knows that he is watching as she's leaving.

GROUPS OF CHILDREN

I was sitting on a barstool at The Doorstop, a place I'd never been. I had to get away, somewhere Robert wouldn't find me. I'd been dating Robert six months—he'd been married until after his baby drowned a year ago. He told me his wife probably killed the baby, but that he drove her to it. I figured it was Robert's way of dealing.

I sipped red wine and smoked a cigarette I bought from the machine far off in the corner. I looked around the bar. The lights were dim, and the air was hazy. There were only a few people at the bar: an older couple on the other end, a man wearing a blue-striped shirt two stools away from me.

The bartender kept asking if I needed more, and I stared at the cowlick in his hairline, which reminded me of Robert, who had one just like it, only on the other side. Robert's hair was thinner, but it was that same brown, same style too almost, bangs flipped, the sides shaved like a military cut. The bartender had nice eyes. I thought about what it would be like to take him home, and the more I thought about it, the more I thought about being with some guy who wasn't Robert. I asked the guy for another glass of wine. Told him my name was Cindy. He grinned at me.

I used to bartend too, and I'd been a dancer, but that was long ago, before I changed my ways, before I became a teacher for disabled kids. Tonight I felt overanxious and excited, like I was on a one-night pass in army basic training.

People started pouring in. The blue-striped shirt guy moved to the chair right next to mine. "You want a drink?" he said.

I smiled at him, and glanced away.

"What's your name?" he said.

I looked at him. "Whatever you want," I said. His eyes were more beautiful than Robert's, sexy in a way. He had a pretty face, nice dimples, and I thought if I was going home with anyone, it would be with him, as long as he didn't have some complicated story. His face was distinct and charming, his skin smooth and baby-like, and his lashes were dark and long, outlining his deep blue eyes like some kind of painting. He looked like a watercolor of an angel.

He told the bartender to get me a drink, to put it on his tab. "I'm Darrell," he said. "You're pretty cute."

"Yeah, whatever," I said, waving him away. "So are you." I laughed and grabbed the wine.

"I mean it," Darrell said. He sipped his Michelob. The place was filling up a little.

"Yeah," I said. I leaned over the counter. "Look, I don't know what you want. If you want to fuck, that's fine, but spare me the patter."

He grinned. "I like to fuck," he said. He touched the back of my neck, rubbing his thumb across it. He smelled like aftershave.

I felt an elbow in my side, so I looked over, saw a drunk woman toppling over, almost falling on the floor. She caught her balance.

Darrell got up to use the bathroom, and I ordered another drink, put it on his tab. When Darrell came back, he said, "Let's pretend we just got married."

"OK," I said. "But first, tell me something funny. I don't care if it's a lie."

"You're really cute," he said.

"Fuck you," I said. "Try again."

It took him a while, and then he said, "My wife divorced me. I got two kids." He took out his wallet and showed me pictures of the kids. I looked through his wallet. Didn't find anything exciting.

"Not funny," I said. "I told you, I don't want any stories."

"You're a bitch," he said.

"Fuck you," I said again. I gave his wallet back.

He put his hand on my leg. I got close, smelling him. He moved his arm, putting it around me. Then he leaned over, kissing me. I told him he didn't ask if he could do that, then I sat back and took a long swallow of wine.

We were in his Jag when he told me he was FBI.

"Please," I said. "Do you have a decent house? I don't want ordinary."

"My wife just left."

"OK, let's try a hotel. A suite, room service, champagne. I don't want to hear about your wife."

"What's up with you and people's problems?" he said.

I looked out the windshield at the traffic light turning yellow. He stopped, waited for the red, then went on green, probably going no faster than the limit. I stared straight ahead, focusing on a sign that looked like a green tack that got bigger as we neared it. I said, "I'm dating this guy. Says his ex-wife killed his baby. He stays glued to the TV, watching the news to see how people drown, always on the Net, checking the latest crime report. Say homicide, and he jumps about ten feet. He watches *Law and Order, NYPD Blue,* anything that has to do with people dying. He even saves them on his tapes. And, every single Sunday, he requests a prayer for his dead baby at our church, although he says there's no reason to believe."

"That's my church," he said.

"Anytime we go to Walmart to get groceries, he lingers in the baby section, touching all the frilly dresses for the two-year-olds. It doesn't help that he sells swimming pools."

The green sign told me we were going toward the airport.

"Sounds awful," Darrell said.

I watched the lights blinking on the pad, the planes taxiing the runway, some ascending, some descending, and I thought about their destinations. I loved to fly, had almost been a pilot, but my ex-husband talked me out of it, saying our marriage would never work if I was always flying off to other countries. I could still fly, I thought, if I really wanted to. But I loved the kids I worked with at the school, where I met Robert, who was a teacher too, until his baby died and then he couldn't stand to be around kids. Now he was selling swimming pools and telling people about unattended children.

I figured Darrell had been lying about being in the FBI, but I went along with it. There was nothing in his wallet that said the FBI. "Tell me about your latest bust," I said.

"Top secret," Darrell said. "If I tell you, I'll have to kill you."

"You're a card, Ralph," I said.

The hotel was booked, so he took me to his place. It was on the upper side of town, near the river, with a huge driveway that was barricaded by an iron-looking fence. He had to unlock it with his remote in order to get in.

"I thought your place wasn't very fancy," I said.

"It's just my ex-wife," he said. "I didn't want to fuck you with all her stuff around."

"Just pretend I'm your prostitute or something."

He laughed, and stopped the car. "Remember, we're faking that we're married."

"Oh yeah," I said. I got out and smelled the flowers that were lined along the lighted walk. They sort of looked like roses. I followed him to the door. "Where we going for our honeymoon?"

"I have some great champagne," he said.

He had to use the bathroom. I walked around, admiring. The ceilings rose high like a cathedral, and the floors were like a creamy marble. The beams could have been cement. I lived in a small a-partment with bare windows and a sofa I bought for twenty bucks at a garage sale. I felt as if I were in a castle, stealing someone else's life for just a moment, like I was a peasant at the Royal Family's home, asking if I could use their phone, worried about getting my dirty hands on their receiver. It made me feel uncomfortable for a minute, but then I thought that just because he had a better place didn't mean that he was any better off.

I went into the kitchen. A Pampers bag sat on his kitchen table and a box of baby wipes was on a chair. Toys were scattered on his floor: a See-N-Say with goofy animal faces smiling in a circle, and some stuffed red-and-yellow clown. They looked really out of place. Darrell came into the kitchen.

"Nice place you got," I said.

"It does its job."

"The FBI really pays its people."

He walked over to the bar and opened the champagne, the cork spinning across the room until it hit a wall. I sat on his fancy counter, he handed me champagne, and then he started smoking.

"I didn't know you smoked," I said.

I held up my Slim and he lit it with the cheapest plastic lighter.

"I didn't know you could be so sexy," he said.

I laughed again. "I'm Bridget," I told Darrell. "You got anything to eat?" I got down from the counter and looked in the fridge, then searched for a glass and poured myself some orange juice. After I finished up my glass, I swirled the carton, mixing up the pulp. There were only sips left so I drank it straight from the container.

"You're kind of cool," he said.

I rummaged in his fridge some more. It was pretty full. I got out a slice of bread and tore off a piece and put it in my mouth. "Let's have sex," I said.

His room was like the rest, except the floors were carpeted with white. It was on the second floor. His bed was in the middle of the room, and it was the biggest bed I'd ever seen, with silky golden sheets. Huge windows took up three sides of the room. The fourth wall was covered with swirls of black-and-blue. Looking down, all I could see was water, the lake that circled the backyard of his home. "This is beautiful," I said.

We kissed, took off our clothes. Darrell wasn't bad. At least he didn't mention his ex-wife while we were fucking. I told Darrell I was pleasantly relieved.

"Jesus," Darrell said, starting up a cigarette. "Who do think I am, some dork?"

"Robert always talks about her. Tells me the things they used to do." I took a drag of Darrell's cigarette.

"Looks to me like you ought to marry him," Darrell said.

I puffed on the smoke. He started another for himself.

I said, "They were married four years, had an eighteen-month-old baby. They'd been fighting, and she was outside with Amanda in the tiny plastic pool with patterns of little fish swimming all across it, and he came outside, asking her where his polka-dotted tie was. Anyway, the wife told him, how would she know, she wasn't the one always leaving stuff on floors, she was tired of cleaning after him, and then he stormed inside, slamming things around, yelling out that he'd be late to his noon meeting. She ran inside, slapping him across the face, telling him that she was tired of his complaining and his bullshit. He pushed her against the wall, and went back to work without his tie, and after she got up and went outside, she found the baby face-down in the pool. She called him at work, but he wasn't there yet, so she left a message, and *then* she called the paramedics."

"God," Darrell said. "Holy Jesus."

"So Robert said it was probably her fault that the baby drowned, that she probably killed it, but he probably drove her to it."

"Fuck," Darrell said, turning to face me. "What if she really did it? I mean, killed the kid on purpose?"

I lay back, staring at the ceiling. I guess I hadn't thought of that, hadn't thought of it at all.

Darrell said, "Or what if it was him?"

I put my hand over my bare stomach. I thought I might be sick.

Darrell said, "That's why he's obsessed."

I heard the ticking of a clock. The room was almost empty except for the bed, and some sculpture in the corner. The art was black and tall, solid, curved, with thin lines spindling in various directions. My head was spinning.

I woke up in his room, and my watch said six a.m. I was naked, alone. I felt a little funny, out of place, so I just closed my eyes and tried falling back asleep.

Darrell came into the room. I wasn't watching, but I could hear his footsteps. He crawled under the sheets. He rubbed against me. He was naked. He blew into my ear. Moved between my legs. Started kissing on my neck. It wasn't a terrible feeling, but it wasn't a thrill, either. I got up and told Darrell I better go. He found his keys and we got dressed, and then he took me back to get my car.

When we got to the lot, he squeezed my leg and wished me luck with Robert. "You know I'm not really FBI. But we can investigate," he said, and winked.

When I got home I found six phone messages from Robert, asking where I'd been. I dropped my purse by the door, and then brushed my teeth. The phone rang, and after I rinsed my mouth, I picked up the cordless. "Cindy," he said. "Where've you been?"

"I went out. I needed time," I said. I slipped off my shoes and put them by the door, then sat on my twenty-dollar sofa.

"For what?" Robert said.

"I met a guy from the FBI. He said he could help with your investigation."

"I have a fever," he said. "I went to the hospital this morning."

"You OK?" I said.

"I missed seeing you," he said. "You could have told me where you were. I sold another pool. Do you mind coming over?"

Robert still lived in the house where his baby died. His wife had wanted to move, but he didn't, so that's one of the reasons why she left him. It was pretty nice, a two-story home with friendly neighbors, always asking how I was when Robert and I passed on our daily walks. He had a fenced backyard, now absent of any pool, of course, but there was enough space if he wanted one. Sometimes we lay in the back, soaking in the sun, eating sub sandwiches on the picnic table, and I would always wonder where his baby Amanda really died, although Robert showed me where the pool had been. I wondered what she had been like alive—I'd seen tons of pictures, watched the videos—I knew her as a ghost, but I didn't know what it was like to touch her skin, and I tried to imagine what she smelled like. I wondered a lot about those things. I'd always wanted children.

He was in bed when I got there. I walked right in, passing the living room where there were baby pictures everywhere, a wall lined with portraits of Amanda. She had cute blonde curls, the prettiest blue eyes just like her father's. I couldn't imagine being blessed with a child as beautiful as she. Her ashes were on the top shelf of the bookcase—there'd been an argument between Robert and his wife over who would get the ashes, so they split them, putting each half in a separate urn.

He was watching *ER*, rewinding the scene of the staff working on a baby.

I sat on the bed. "How're you feeling?"

He was sweaty, looking sort of pasty, dark bags under his big eyes. It was hard for me to see a guy as tall and fit as Robert looking so pathetic. "I'm really sick," he said. "My temp is 104."

I leaned and kissed his forehead.

"Tell me about this guy," he said.

I took off my shoes, and crawled under the covers. I faced him, lying on my side. I said, "We had sex."

Robert turned away from me, moved closer to the edge. "How could you?" he said.

I shifted to my back, stared up at the ceiling. "I don't know."

"Jesus, Cindy."

"I'm sorry," I said, facing Robert. "I don't know what happened."

He turned toward me, moving close, staring at me for a minute, then he ran his thumb over my chin. "It's OK," he said. He frowned. "Maybe I drove you to it."

A train rolled by in the distance. It sounded like an airplane.

On Sunday, we went to church as usual. The church was almost like the one I'd gone to as a kid, with the varnished wooden pews, the Jesus portrait with outstretched arms up behind the altar, the cream-colored tiles on the floor, and the organ sounds used to make me feel as if I were in heaven, at least that's what I'd imagined. I loved turning the crispy hymnal pages, and the church usually smelled like pine, and whomever I was sitting next to. It used to be a place for me to get away, forget about the troubles of the world, where I believed that there were things beyond my little life. Now I didn't know what church meant.

But looking at the pastor preaching in the pulpit in his faded robe, I thought about Amanda. I had an eerie feeling. I looked at Robert. A baby cried. Robert squeezed my hand.

As we sat in the pew and listened to the sermon, I glanced in the next row, and I saw someone familiar. It was Darrell. His profile was clear and as he turned his head, I could see the bright blue of his eye, the slight tilt of his upper lip. He bowed his head, and it looked like he was praying. I wondered if he was having any luck.

I prayed. I remembered how I felt as a kid, and I sort of felt that now, sort of small, but still worth something. I remembered what it was like having faith. I wanted to hold onto that same feeling, but I knew as soon as church was over I'd forget.

After the service, in the lobby, Darrell walked up to me and Robert. "Hi," I said to Darrell.

"Bridget," Darrell said, holding out his hand.

Robert looked taller next to Darrell, who was about my height. "Bridget?" Robert said.

"Cindy," I said to Darrell. "My name is really Cindy."

I introduced the men, and they shook hands. I told Robert that Darrell was the FBI guy who said he could help us out.

"Want to go somewhere for coffee?" Robert said.

IHOP was pretty packed, so we settled for nonsmoking. The skin of my legs stuck to the seat of the booth. Robert sat across from

Darrell, and we all ordered coffee and blueberry muffins and they also ordered omelets. I drank my coffee black and so did Darrell, and Robert added tons of cream. He blew on his cup, lifting it to his chin, some coffee spilling on his saucer, the cream dribbling on the wobbly bluish table. The waitress in her pink dress cleaned it up.

"So, tell me," Robert said. "You're in the FBI?"

Darrell wiped his lips with a napkin. There was a crumb left on his chin, next to a tiny scar I hadn't noticed. "I hear you had some troubles with your wife," Darrell said.

I put my hands around my cup, looking at the marks my lipstick left. I glanced at Robert, then at Darrell, who placed a portion of his omelet on his fork.

Robert swallowed, looked at me, took a sip of water. He sighed, then sighed again. "I don't want to file charges," Robert said. "I just want your opinion."

"Can do," Darrell said.

Silverware clinked from the nearby tables, muffled voices all around, the waitress asking a man in the next booth if he wanted extra sugar.

Robert moved his plate out of the way, put his coffee next to mine, and he leaned into Darrell. Robert grabbed my hand, lifting it up to the table, locking our fingers together as if they were in prayer.

"My ex-wife," Robert said. "She told me that she was so mad at me, she put Amanda's head under the water and watched her gasp for breath. She said if I told, she'd say *I* did it. It probably was my fault for being such a shitty husband."

Darrell looked at me, then looked back at Robert.

"Really?" I said to Robert.

Robert looked at me. "Yeah," he said.

"Uh-huh," Darrell said, putting down his fork.

"Well, what do you think I should do? I don't think she really did it. I mean, she's probably just trying to guilt trip me."

"Robert," I said.

"He's FBI, right?"

Robert put his hand over my shoulder, fingering my strap. He said to Darrell, "How well do you know Cindy?"

I looked at Robert.

"Not that well," Darrell said. "All I did was fuck her." He waved both hands, then got up and walked away.

Robert opened up my car door, then got in on his side. He said, "That was stupid." He started up the car, pulled out of the lot.

He put a stick of Big Red in his mouth.

I looked at the trees that we passed by, the wind shifting crispy leaves in every direction.

I thought about everything he said.

I said, "It really wasn't."

Far off, I saw a group of children. They played. They sang. They laughed.

VICTOR

Victor, the ship, moves with his nose forward, the upward side of him in the shape of a pumpkin.

When he starts to sink, people in him make an exodus, their bodies pushing, jumping, making every effort to get the hell out of him.

THE COOKIE ROOM

Mandy's husband, Brian, turned her master sergeant in for making a pass at her. They were in the Air Force, worked in a hospital lab, and her master sergeant was Raymond Taylor. Mandy was a sergeant, twenty-eight, working in the blood bank and Brian was a captain and worked in chemistry. While dating, they had to keep things quiet since he was an officer and she wasn't and that was illegal fraternization. A week after they were married, Mandy slept with a guy named Paul, who also worked in the blood bank.

She never told Brian about that, nor about any of her history, because she didn't know how he'd react. Mandy was afraid if he found out that she'd been raped before she met him, and then slept around after that, he'd never have married her.

While Mandy was doing blood types, shaking clear glass tubes, holding them up to the light to check for agglutination, out of the corner of her eye she saw a figure, and smelled cologne, and she knew it was Sergeant Taylor.

He carried heavy boxes of saline. Sweat beaded on his forehead. He put the boxes down, then hooked up the saline to the cell washers. "That should take care of you for a while," he said.

He put his hands on her back, and she could smell his perspiration. "I've got something special planned for you before I go away," he said. He had orders to Greece, and would be taking his whole family.

As he left the room, another blood banker, Krista, entered the department, putting on her lab coat—Krista was red-haired, skinny, with a blotchy scarred complexion.

"Welcome back," said Mandy.

"You run today?" Krista said, putting on a pair of gloves.

"Just a short one," Mandy said, grabbing an O from the fridge so she could do a crossmatch. She usually went running on her lunch breaks, since anyone who worked out during lunch got extra time. Sometimes Krista and Mandy would run around the flight line, where there was a lot of open space.

Sometimes while Krista and Mandy ran, they talked about someday having kids. Mandy wasn't sure if she wanted children, but Brian wanted to start a family, and she guessed since he was a good husband, he'd be a decent father. For the past few months, since Mandy had agreed to go off birth control, Brian seemed so happy. She tested herself once a week, and the signs were always negative. She didn't tell him about the abortion she'd had after she was raped. There were a lot of things she'd kept so quiet, sometimes she had to try to figure out if they were real, or if she'd seen them in a movie, or read about them in a book.

Since the guy who had worked weekends got orders, for the first time since she'd been there she was working on a weekend. It was Saturday and she was in the cookie room, the place where blood donors replenished their bodies after giving blood. She was eating with Brian, since he'd brought her a Subway six-inch like he always did when she was working. Since it was a weekend, the donor room was closed and no one else was there.

"Who's the supervisor today?" Brian asked.

"Taylor." She tore her sandwich in squares.

"There's a slacker for you," Brian said. He put down his sub and came up behind her and put his arms around her. They started making out.

"Easy there, girl," he said. "We can finish when you get home."

"Thanks, pal," she said, dumping her sub in the trash bin.

Sergeant Taylor didn't come in Saturday, but Sunday, while she was thawing fresh frozen plasma for a patient, standing by the plasma microwave, she heard footsteps, and smelled the strong cologne he always wore.

"Busy?" he said.

"Not bad," she said. After she finished with the units, she scrubbed down all the counters.

"I'm going to miss you when I leave," he said. "I'm buying you something special so you'll remember me."

"You don't have to do that," she said.

"Come to the cookie room. I have something to show you."

Mandy followed him, going past the donor room, past the rows of chairs, to the cookie room, which was tucked away in back. He stopped and sat down in a chair, and she sat across from him, crossing her legs.

"So," she said. "You going to give me my evaluation?"

"That was last month, remember? I was hoping for something else," he said.

She looked at him and he didn't seem so bad. She noticed his lips, so dark and full, and that made her wonder what it would be like to kiss them. He smiled, and she watched his mouth curve up and stretch across his teeth, and then she saw a small crumb on his chin, so she leaned over, getting close as she brushed his skin with her index finger.

"You have a crumb," she said, then got up and fetched a napkin from the counter. The napkin dropped down to the floor. She bent down and threw it in the trashcan and got another one, handing it to him.

He got up and hovered over her and looked down at her face.

"You're pretty," he said, touching a long strand that had fallen from her ponytail. She felt the roughness of his finger on her cheekbone.

She knew what was happening, knew he was coming on to her, that she'd encouraged him. Then she thought maybe he was being nice, that he knew she loved attention, and maybe he felt sorry for a girl like her, and knew she needed reassurance. She knew she better stop herself, so she turned her head away and said, "I better not."

He backed off and opened a box of Chips Ahoy and took a bite, and she noticed his big hands, and she studied his face, and she felt sorry for him in some pathetic kind of way and she tried to think of what to say, but there was this uncomfortable silence and he just looked at her while chewing on his cookie. He smiled and said, "Hope I get some of you before I leave," then passed her and walked out the door and left the lab. She spent most of the day in this trance that made work fast and almost fun, wondering if he was coming back.

That night, she felt like making love. She got naked and went into Brian's office in the den, where he was sitting behind his desk, typing on his keyboard.

"Make love to me," she said.

"In a bit," he said, staring at his screen.

She stood at the door. She stayed there. But he kept on working.

She thought about what happened earlier that day. She said, "Sergeant Taylor tried kissing me today."

Brian stopped what he was doing. "You're kidding," he said, looking up. "Why would he do a thing like that?"

"Maybe he thinks I'm cute," she said, walking down the hallway. She heard Brian's footsteps following behind her.

On Monday, she was off. She was picking weeds from the garden, and Brian came home from lunch, hopping out of the Intrepid. He stepped up, staying on the grass. "I told Major Vargas about Taylor," he said, hands tucked in his pockets. "He wants you in ASAP." Vargas was Sergeant Taylor's boss.

"Why'd you do that?" she said. She picked up the hoe that had been lying on the ground and started chopping. "Jesus." She hoed harder and deeper, then stopped, looking up at him. "That was really dumb, you know that?"

"It's the rules," he said. "You know how that works."

She brushed the dirt from her clothes, then marched to the house.

He watched her as she got ready to hop into the shower. He said, "You're not cheating on me, are you?" he said.

She sat next to him and squeezed his hand. "No," she said. "You know I'd never do that."

Major Vargas told her to write down everything that happened, talk to the commander, and file a complaint at Social Actions, the place that promoted equal opportunity and dealt with discrimination and sexual harassment.

After Major Vargas called Social Actions and told them to expect her, she walked across base, where a man sat behind a desk, papers in front of him. "Every detail," he said. He got up and pointed to the bottom of the sheet. "Sign down at the bottom."

"What happens if I don't?" she said.

"It's you or him," he said.

The Social Actions guy paced across the floor, rubbing his fingers over his moustache. "If you don't do it, you'll be reprimanded."

As Mandy sat staring at the paper, clicking the end of the pen, she listened to the boards vibrating under his shiny combat boots, and then she wrote, "Maybe Taylor was going to kiss me. But I don't know, I could be wrong."

Then she had to see the Chief, the guy in charge of the lab. After she told him it was absolutely nothing, he leaned forward, and she thought he was going to spit right in her face. He said, "When I first joined the Air Force, women weren't allowed. You can't go crying just because some guy wants to kiss you."

"Tell that to my jerk of a husband," she said. She crossed her arms, staring at a scuffmark on the tip of her white shoe.

The next day, Krista and Mandy ran around the flight line. The airplane fumes were potent and made Mandy feel alive, just like the smell of coffee. Big C5s and wicked fighter jets descended, and she imagined jumping high enough to touch them—when the planes took off, she'd get depressed for just a second, wanting to hang onto a wing and fly along. They were like powerful, angry gods compared to the birds who seemed so delicate and sweet. Sometimes, if she ran long enough, she'd get a runner's high that made her feel like she was flying.

Now the ground was wet, and it smelled like spring. Sprinkles fell onto Mandy's face, into her hair.

After a couple miles, since Krista asked again, Mandy told her what had happened with Sergeant Taylor, telling her the same things she'd written on the form at Social Actions, leaving out the parts she really wanted.

"He's a jerk," Krista said between puffy breaths, her blue Nikes pounding on the pavement. "I'm glad he never hit on me."

"I wonder why he didn't," Mandy said, stopping to tie her laces. After she finished the knot, she got up and ran again, catching up to Krista.

"I'm not exactly Miss America," Krista said. "Mandy, look at you. Blonde. Big boobs, tiny waist. You're a walking Barbie doll screaming out for sex."

"He could be exciting, don't you think?" Mandy listened to the rhythm of their breathing, unsynchronized: like the cadence of day one in basic training. "Brian's the one who turned him in, you know."

Mandy wasn't supposed to talk about what happened, but everyone at work knew. It went on for weeks, people stopping her in the lab, asking her about it. Every now and then, Chief would call her to his office to give her some lecture about the military, saying he had connections and a lot of power, so she'd just sit there feeling helpless, trying to take his talk. Sometimes he'd stop by the blood bank, telling her that she was out of regulation, that her ponytail was too long or her dress was too short and if he had to tell her one more time, he'd write her up for bad appearance.

Her pregnancy tests were always negative, and she and Brian were fighting all the time. He said if she wasn't such a tease, all this stuff with Sergeant Taylor wouldn't have happened.

And then, a few weeks after all this stuff started, Krista said her husband had found a record on Sergeant Taylor from six years ago at a base in Guam for harassing a co-worker. And now there were rumors going around that he'd hit on other girls who worked in the lab, asking them for sexual favors, paying them with days off and other things. Mandy wondered why he never went that far with her.

That night, when she was hoeing again, Brian was on the porch, sitting on a chair. She stopped what she was doing and sat across from him, pulling her knees up to her chest. She studied his curls, at the sunset glowing on them that made them shine in certain places. He was quiet, staring at the floor.

"Something wrong?" she said.

He shook his head and said "no."

"I can tell when something's wrong," she said.

"I was passed up for promotion because of this stuff with you and Taylor."

She said, "That's fucked up for you to say that."

Brian raised his fist. He said, "It's not my fault. And it isn't all his either."

"Fuck you," she said, getting up. "If I wanted I could fuck him. At least he'd give me that." She marched into the house, letting the screen door slam behind her.

The next night, Brian was at the gym playing basketball while Mandy was at home, baking cookies. She found Sergeant Taylor's number in the book, then picked up the cordless. He answered the phone, and she told him she was sorry for everything that happened.

"Doesn't matter," he said.

"Maybe we can talk about it?" She grabbed a cookie from the sheet and it was still soft and warm, so a corner broke and she blew on it, then put it in her mouth and sucked on it, savoring the chocolate.

He gave her directions to his house, so she left a note for Brian, telling him she'd gone to get more eggs, and she went to Sergeant Taylor's.

After she arrived, he didn't talk about the trial, or about the report she had to file, but he invited her inside, and right away, he kissed her. They went to his bedroom. Most of the time she closed her eyes, but when she opened them, she was reminded of who she was really with, which fascinated her, and she'd smile at him and then he'd smile back and squint his eyes and ooh and aah, and it was then she knew she had him.

And after he came inside of her, he reached over to his nightstand and lit a cigarette, then handed it to her. She inhaled the Kool, then gave it back, laying on her side, her big toe tickling his calves.

"For a girl as quiet as you, you're pretty good," he said. "Surprising."

It was the same thing Brian had said once.

"Gee," she said, turning on her back and spreading out.

"I never thought you'd sleep with me," he said.

"Why's that?" she said, staring at a cobweb hanging from the ceiling.

"I'm no Casanova," he said.

She turned toward him and he put the smoke out in the flimsy ashtray that looked like it was from McDonald's. He reached over and enveloped her as if she were a fragile letter that carried an honest, heartfelt message. She liked the way he touched her. He made her feel like she was special. He held his hand up to her face and ran his fingers through her hair and smiled at her and told her she was pretty. She got close, and buried herself in his arms, then closed her eyes and felt his warmth against her cold and shivering body. They lay there for a while in silence, and she knew she had to go home.

She got up, dressed, watching herself in the mirror of Sergeant Taylor's dresser. She straightened her hair, rearranging her curls with the tips of her long fingers. She touched up the mascara under her pale eyes, and traced her lips with the red gloss from her purse. She turned to the side, eyeing her figure, and she asked Sergeant Taylor if she looked OK.

He said she looked too good to be true.

THE YELLOW GLITTERY ONE

One guy's voice was nasal-like, she noticed. His nails were brittle and his skin looked like paper.

Another one comes over in, as she discovers—just his flight suit and nothing else. He flies rescue helicopters, has worked for the hospital where she worked once.

They fuck.

At her place, another time, he brings out one dildo, then the next.

He says, "Try this one. Try this one."

"The yellow glittery one!" she says

It's an awful lot for her to keep up with.

And he's already showed her pictures of his home built of stone with varnished logs decorating it at random angles—with its high ceilings, sinks like bowls, windows shaped like tulips—where he says his is certain she'll fit right in.

She met the most recent man at the café. They hugged and he smelled like a banana.

WHAT TO DO ON VACATION

Aye-Aye
As she calls him, hearing the ring, she thinks about the lemurs they might see, the ring-tailed and the red-ruffed and the aye-aye, their tails like felines, their bulging eyes, their faces like rodents. Hearing their calls, a grasshoppered chant.

For her spring break, which is in two weeks, he offered to take her anywhere, since, on her reprieves from teaching, she'd been the one to drive states across to see him. He has a new job at a bank, which means he hardly has vacation. Ring, ring, and she's been wanting to go to Madagascar if just to see the lemurs, so he booked a flight, reserving a hotel, saying he'll go as long as they could have some fun.

She reaches his voicemail, clears her throat and says: I want to chat. Glad to have used the word "chat" because "talk" sounds too official, and she knows how he likes to avoid anything more than a chat.

She puts her lunch noodles away, hearing the bong from the church on the corner, meaning maybe it's the hour. She's been trying to pass the time—sitting with applications from students wanting to get into the program where she teaches—she's been staring at the numbers on the wall clock. Something inside her has been nagging for a while, and just the day before, on her way to teach, it hit her, she knew what she had to say, and she knew she had to say it, and then the day passed, and then today became today and now she knows she can't spend any more time with the weight of it'

She looks out the window down into the courtyard at a patch of snow, knowing soon it will be gone again. The sky is gray like usual and the cars along the street really haven't changed much—the maintenance guy's Jeep with its independence logos—he's asked her out a few times and she doesn't say she has a boyfriend, just maybe she can make it, but then she makes up any reason not to, like she has a work reception, or she has to Skype her mother, her friend Lucy, or her sister. She's an only child. She always wanted a sister.

She's only seen lemurs in books, heard their voices on recordings, which she sometimes falls asleep to. She grew up on a farm. She knows a lot about animals.

She gets out a stick of incense, puts it in its holder and flicks the lighter. She takes in the sandalwood scent, like she keeps taking in his promises. This man of promise, at least sometimes coming through, unlike the boy he was in high school, only then he'd only promised to call her back. Since last year, after reuniting, it's a future with houses and yards and fancy cars and maybe even children.

She hears the phone and when she sees it's him, she lets it ring four times before deciding to answer.

Sassypants

He stops his paint job to call, asking did you call me? She says yes and how are you and he tells her he's painting the kitchen. She sounds like she's been crying. He figures it's probably that time of the month again.

Now she's saying she's scared about vacation, something about her needs and he starts tuning out until he hears her say something about his drinking again. That really gets to him. She's says something about lemurs. Sometimes on the phone, she'll play them for him on the speaker. Though he doesn't tell her, he thinks that's kind of weird. Once as a joke, he said they sound like chipmunks.

He'd like to see a panther himself, and now, on the phone, she's asking all about their future, how he's only been to see her once. She says he made a promise.

What promise? he says, which seems to make her cry even harder.

He says, I've been to see you.

He's taken all of his vacation, has driven hours to the airport, got on the plane to her state of New York, which he's never really liked much.

He lifts his brush, smelling something clove-like. He remembers a dead toad she found that summer in his driveway. She picked it up with her bare hands and plopped it on the table like his dog would. Now she's talking about yoga and the backbend, how she's trying to be healthy, and is he eating better like he promised? Like that day they made a pact? The paint smell is getting to him, and he has to finish his improvements if he'll ever feel good about having to go back to work again on Monday.

He looks at the ceiling of his house, which he did up for Elle's last visit—new carpets and cabinets and refinished hardwood floors—and all she could say then was how are you going to sell this when you move with me to New York? Remember, like you'd promised?

He starts getting dizzy and he doesn't know what she's talking about. It's really getting on his nerves, and so he says that.

You Can Do Anything
Of course he's defensive. She lets him go, when he says he has to. She lets the phone charge, kind of disappointed in herself for not being more assertive. She keeps telling him, I'm trying to be honest. She's said that to other guys before. Every day, she says that to herself.

Bells chime. She gets tired of that too, so she puts on headphones, hearing lemurs, letting their sound soothe her. She lies on the ground in dead pose.

When she wakes, she calls her friend Lucy who used to be her teacher. The woman is retired with the same name and age of her mother, who left when Elle was a toddler.

It didn't go so well, she says.

Lucy says, I'm sorry. She mentions her plans to buy a bigger, better house. She's been single most her life, save a few boyfriends who she says never really did much.

Homemade

His paint job is ruined. He sees a trickle in the corner, a floundering shade of yellow and he doesn't know how it got there. He notices a yellow spot above the sink, one over the stovetop. He thought he painted it all white, and there's no yellow on his paintbrush. He puts the thing down on the tray and goes to the fridge for a beer, thinking his anger makes him see things, infuriated how his girlfriend—on the phone—can just seem sweet one hour, and the next, call him weeping saying that she's scared now.

He goes out to smoke with his back to the window, surveying the melting snow, thinking he'll maybe plant a garden when the time comes, with tomatoes and carrots and possibly peppers. He can make his salsa. He exhales his smoke and thinks of Scarlet, the girl at the bar the week before, her calloused face on his when she said she was affordable. He never cheated on his girlfriend. He doesn't remember a whole lot about Scarlet besides the fact that she made him laugh.

He gets another beer from the fridge, then looks inside the crisper, finding nothing but an apple probably left from when Elle was visiting for Christmas. She stayed the whole month. He doesn't remember much about the wee hours she arrived—besides her waking him from a dream about rams and pigeons and international sliders.

He gets out a knife and cuts the apple. It's soggy and rotten. He examines its mushy core and plucks the seeds out. He puts them on a plate. He doesn't eat much fruit. He's mostly allergic.

He has another beer, and notices the whole room seems yellow. His eyes hurt, so he goes to the living room. It's dark, its walls a dull green that also need repainting. He remembers telling this to Elle one December day after work. He saw her on the far end of the sofa, typing on her laptop.

Now he's surprised she hasn't called yet to say she's sorry.

As the sun begins to fade, he isn't sure how many beers he'll have to go yet. He grabs another, sipping. Contemplating, then another. He turns on the iPod and the speakers, to a tune he and his brother used to blast on the road on their way to the rodeos in Texas. How the bull would try to buck him. He's been a champion. He calls his brother and after only getting voicemail, he sits on the far end of the sofa and puts his feet up. He closes his eyes and sees a yellow sun, the face of his ex-wife, a beach with lizards and rum.

Tree

Elle does the Tree Pose. She stands upright on the toe stand, and feels iffy on the Rabbit, hard to see herself with her head tucked.

She makes soup with the pulp from her juicer, adding nutmeg, cinnamon and cayenne, letting the smells fill the space in her apartment. On the fridge she looks at the picture of Mike's niece's kindergarten smile, the girl reminding Elle so much of herself when she was her age.

On the fridge, the girl's construction paper card says thank you and I love you, with their cursive slants. Elle can almost hear the young girl's voice. How that girl embraced her.

At the computer, Elle looks at pictures of Mike, when he'd come to see her that one time and they drove to The Falls. The place known for honeymoons. It's one of the Great Wonders. To her, it's never far. She's gone with lots of men. She prefers going on her own, favoring the American side, where she can walk along the river, watching geese as they fly, stopping on a rock and staying put there. Sometimes she sits on a bench and closes her eyes to hear the rush and spill.

She writes a little in her journal, first about her boyfriend's ChapStick, his stashes in the glove box and the kitchen. At the bedside, by the toilet. He has moist lips. At their trip once to a mountain that didn't seem like a mountain, where he said he was a ranger. There was gin on his breath. He insisted on driving them around the bends and down down down and back to his home where—even though at that time was a rental—he painted all the rooms and did the floor up, saying he specialized in homes and fix-work, his expertise in markets and mortgage and all that complicated bank stuff.

She remembers their first kiss. That night he walked her home after she met him at a party that ended when the cops came. How nice she thought that was then. He was your first, she says to herself. Wake up! She isn't sixteen anymore.

Rodeo

He feels like dancing. *King of the Road.* He moves his feet and re-members his brother driving the Cavalier with their vests and chaps and hats. Jamie is the youngest and came down to live with Mike in Kansas after their father disappeared again. Jamie was sixteen and Mike was in college on a rodeo scholarship. Mike made his name in bareback—until that day that he doesn't remember much of besides the hoards of people with their hands, their mouths, the doctor with his glasses.

Animal

The Falls make everyone seem tiny. In Elle's pictures, Mike stands by a rail. He's bald, his face rosy. His eyes are blue.

She compares her shots. Dimitri was a pianist from Cyprus who taught her how to cook from the produce in his garden. She looks at his smooth skin and his Armani blazer and remembers their shopping trips to San Francisco, her sitting by the mirror while he came out to show her his outfits. Don was a hairy famous man she'd met at a conference in Chicago, who she'd asked to be her mentor. He lived in another state, and sent her so many gifts, she got to know the UPS guy. After he said he'd be in town and asked to meet her at the Falls, she agreed to meet him on a bench.

As they walked he took her hand and asked if they could kiss. She's kissed a lot of guys. She thinks of her father, who died of a heart attack last year. It was just one month before Mike looked her up again and found her.

She decides to go the movies, watching whatever is playing when she gets there.

King

Mike's brother Jamie finally calls. Oh, hoy! Mike says, and he hears his brother's laughter. His brother's rodeo days have left his back and knees disabled. He's unemployed, though Mike is pretty sure he can find work if he's desperate. King of the rodeo, he says.

Oy-hoy, says Jamie. He says Florida is cooking. His lady has a new job at the golf course. He says, The one at Mom and Tom's place.

Their *other* place, says Mike. They'll never leave Wisconsin.

Mike talks to Jamie for a while about Elle. He says, I can't figure out what's up. She's probably bleeding again.

Hold your rope, Jamie says. She's always been a good one.

Bridesmaids

Elle goes to the bathroom and listens to the message. Mike's voice is curt and distant, not calling her any of those pet names. In the mirror, she tries to laugh like the women in the movie. Between her teeth, she sees a shell of popcorn, finds the floss from her handbag, digs it out. She goes back to her seat in the dark, where someone makes the sound of a hyena.

Sixty Minutes

Mike wakes up the next morning on the sofa in his street clothes, to a phone ring.

He asks her what she's up to.

Coffee, she says, and my usual morning toast.

The blinds are shut. He squints. He asks her the time.

She says, Here, I have ten-thirty. I was at a movie last night. It was funny.

You went alone? he says.

On the way to the kitchen, he finds a stick of Big Red. He puts it in his mouth. He applies his Cherry ChapStick. He sees he left the lid off the paint can. The walls look white. On the floor, he thinks he sees a chigger like from his rodeo days, sleeping on other cowboys' sofas. He can almost feel the heat again, rising to his head, spreading to his toes and to the ends of his pinkies.

Elle says something about balance.

He tells her he loves her. He wants to smell her so bad he feels it in his gut. Though he's not sure why, he says to her, "I'm sorry."

He pictures her curled maybe on her bed, or possibly her sofa—her place is so small she doesn't have too many choices. He wants to ask if she is having her monthly visitor again or whatever else she calls it. Then he figures that should wait. Yes, he thinks. He's better off to save that.

She starts going on, now about hyenas.

Root

She goes to the fridge and slices a pumelo. Puts one half in a bowl, spooning out the insides. It's sweeter than a grapefruit, a descendent of the orange, and certainly plumper. It's also called a lusho, a jabong. She thinks Wikipedia is awesome.

She turns on the TV, finding a show about hyenas. They look so cat-and-dog like. Pretty, almost, with calloused feet and nails, used for turning sharp and hunting. They are mostly nocturnal. Aardwolves, striped and spotted. There's a myth of stealing live-stock, graves, and children. They eat meat. She is finished with her fruit now. Hit the spot, she says to maybe the man on the TV, to herself, or to maybe the hyena. She can find them, if she wants, in Africa and Asia.

When the show is over, she goes back to her lemurs, playing her recording. She chants for a while before turning off her tape and googling to find more about the sounds of the hyena. They seem to giggle and gobble. Like gargling her mouthwash. At night, they howl, wolf-like.

When the phone rings and she sees again it's Mike, she lets it ring and gets on all fours on her floor mat. She tucks her chin, pulls in her abs and curves her spine up.

She keeps her eyes alert. She inhales again, contracts. With a hiss, she howls and roars.

POOFY

"This is a masterpiece," she said to her parrot.

The parrot said, "Masterpiece."

She took the hummus from the blender and spooned it into a small ceramic bowl she'd made at the studio, where the owner's toddler giggled every time she entered, pointing to her poofy orange hair, her earmuffs like two attached potatoes.

On the TV, a player scored a touchdown, and she said, "No way." She was rooting for the Packers.

Her parrot said, "Touchdown."

She put the hummus on the table for her guests who would start arriving in exactly seven minutes.

She washed the blender, turned around to see her dog at the table, eating from the bowl. He looked up with his bulging dark eyes, his head tilted. He'd eaten all the hummus.

The parrot said, "Touchdown."

The dog crouched and the parrot said, "Touchdown. Touchdown. Touchdown."

PHYSICS

I sat there on the floor, reading about red cells for my thesis. My cat Patches was curled at my feet. My boyfriend, William, had come over, we were trying things again, and now I listened as he talked to my son, Jamie, about his job as a reporter. Jamie nodded, more interested in the TV, where some guy was smacking his guitar and double leaping.

My mother called. It was almost Christmas.

"Eileen," my mother said. "Come and see your stepdad."

"What should I say?"

"He loves you, you know."

Patches rubbed my leg. She was calico. I petted her and she started purring. There was silence on my mom's end.

"I'm saying maybe you should come now," she said. "At least think about it."

Her voice began to waver. She started crying, she said she wished it wasn't such a drive for me to see her. I mouthed to William it was my mom. He was making faces at Jamie. Patches scurried to the bedroom.

When I hung up, William told me about a girl he'd known since high school, a girl I'd met in Physics. She was leaving her husband.

"Her problems were that bad?" I said to William.

"One of those marriages that just *look* good," he said.

Miles from next door came over, asking if Jamie could play. He was an older kid who I relied on to babysit. I waved at Jamie as he headed for the door. I sat close to William. He made me feel wanted, just sitting with him.

"Marriage sucks, huh?" he said. He looked at me and started going for something between my teeth with a fingernail.

"It's my stepdad," I said.

"Your mom?" He looked at his watch. He was on his way to a dinner party with this woman. Her name was Anna. He'd just come from the gym, said he should be getting ready.

"Can I come?" I said.

"What about your thesis?" he said.

"I can help," I said. I knew about divorce.

"I guess," he said. "It's your choice."

I called Miles's mother, asked if Miles could stay with Jamie. Then I got dressed and William came and watched, helped me pick an outfit.

I stood there naked, going through my closet. I pulled out a slinky shirt that was falling off a hanger.

"You wearing that?" he said.

I put the shirt back and he got off the bed, rubbing against me. I turned around and let him kiss me but told him the rest could wait. I filtered through my rack, picked out a dress with an embroidered collar.

"You're OK with Shirley Temple?" he said. He took it, put it back, and grabbed the silver top. He told me to show my stuff.

"This one's going to Salvation," I said, taking it from him.

He talked me into my low-rider jeans, that top—the whole outfit showed my navel and my cleavage. I wore boots. All the time I was dressing he was touching me. It was hard to keep my mind on my business. I put on hoops, said, "You go for the sleazy look, huh?"

"Whatever," he said. "It's you."

He slapped my butt, said, "Some women would die to carry off this look."

I tapped his cheek. "Hands off until later. You're kind of reminding me of my *dad*."

He put his arms around me and rocked, and though he didn't always say the right things, I felt a little warm there.

As he showered, I found Jamie outside, shooting baskets with Miles and the neighbor boys. I yelled to them that I was going out.

"Man, with that dork?" Miles said. "You must be hard up."

"Just take care of my son," I said. I kissed Jamie and told him to be good. I watched him try a free throw.

In the car, William put in a CD by Madonna, something we listened to when we were fucking.

"Bring back memories?" he said.

We were the first ones at the party. The table was set with fancy silver dishes and candles burning in the center, the lighting to match. It looked nice in a TV soap opera way.

Other guests arrived. There were about ten in all, and I'd met most of them before at other times with William. They were his friends. I sat on the couch, William next to me, and I rubbed my hand along the cushions—soft, covered in velour—as they all laughed about stuff. I took off my boots, left them sitting on the hardwood. I sat on my feet.

When the group broke up, William put his hand on my back and looked at me.

"What're you thinking?" he said.

"I'm going to stay here," I said.

"What, in this apartment?"

"No, I mean in town. I'm not going north to see my stepdad."

"Oh," he said, sipping his wine, looking toward the kitchen where three of the women were laughing loud about something.

When Anna got there, I gave her a hug. "Hard times, huh?" I said.

She took a long swallow.

She went into the kitchen. I returned to the sofa. William edged closer, his hand on my shoulder. He smelled like my shampoo.

"You know," he said, dropping his hand to my leg. "When I was in the shower I promised myself I'm not touching you tonight. You look so hot. It's like sex cheapens our relationship, or something."

"You're *so* sweet," I said, staring down at something.

"You know what I mean," he said. "You want to stop at my place?"

Dinner was all green, lettuce just like grass, and vegetarian lasagna. Red wine to match the green, as if it were Christmas. William looked at my plate. "Two servings," he said.

"Of everything," I said.

"Like you're Ethiopian."

After a while, I excused myself, taking my glass with me to the bathroom.

Everything was pink. I looked at myself in the mirror and dabbed my lipstick. I looked for floss and did my teeth. I arranged my hair. I looked in the cabinet for gel. Then I heard knocking.

"Can I?" said the woman.

I opened the door and found Anna. I told her I was looking for something for my hair. She reached in her purse, gave me this wax thing.

I said, "Like a hair commercial."

She shut the door. "Bill thought you were sick," she said.

"Paranoid?" I said, doing my hair.

"He just cares," she said.

She sat on the toilet and peed. "You two look good together."

After the meal, we all cleared the table. I sat next to William on the sofa. I kept telling him that he looked really tired. He told me he was energetic, thinking of us going back to his place.

"Should we leave?" he said. I told him whenever he was ready.

The hostess was out of wine, and William had more at home, so he decided we should get some. Anna followed in her car, so she could bring the stuff back to the party.

At William's, I sat on the sofa, petting his dog Baby. Anna sat next to me. William went to the kitchen and Anna talked about her husband.

"He'll fight?" I said.

"For everything," she said.

From the kitchen, William called for Baby.

"What about the kids?" I said.

William came back with the bottle. He looked at Anna, asked

her what it was now. He sat next to her and put his hand on her leg, said that she could stay there.

"You don't have to go back," he said. He went back to the kitchen with the wine, returned with three full glasses and some tissues. Baby trailed behind him. William sat between us, handed out the wine and gave Anna his big tissues.

"It's just me," she said. She took off her glasses. We all sipped our wine. Baby got up and sat on the blanket in the corner.

"Is it time?" William said to her. "Are you ready to come out now?"

She put on her glasses, sipped.

I took some of my own wine.

William put his arms around us. "There's something she wants to tell you," he said. He smiled a little.

He leaned over and he kissed her. I didn't really know what to do. They kept on kissing so I nudged him. That wasn't helping.

"Hey," I said, finally getting up then.

I said to them, "Hello?"

They finally stopped and William looked at me, wiping his saliva. His chin was red. "A threesome would be nice," he said.

Baby started barking.

I went to the kitchen to get a glass of water.

As William drove, he told me he'd been waiting to be alone with me. I told him to just shut up about it.

I started thinking of my stepdad. If he was really as sick as my mother made him sound then.

I told William that was a terrible thing to do with Anna. I said, "She's having a hard time already."

We sat there at a stoplight. I talked about my stepdad. I said I had to go there.

"Do what you want," he said. "How much longer does he have now?"

I looked out the window at the streetlights, at a cat that lurked.

William grabbed my hand. "Can you do that thing?" he said.

"Fuck," I said.

"C'mon," he said. "It's fun."

"You have some nerve," I said. "I was bringing up my family."

He said, "Maybe you'll feel better."

I thought about the night we got back together, the night he said he missed me and wanted more than something sexual. I really wanted that, wanted something deep and lasting, although I wasn't desperate.

I undid his belt, unzipped, reached under his boxers. I sucked on all his fingers, moving in the way I knew to tease him.

He told me that he loved me. He said he was sorry. He said he just wanted to be good to me.

"OK," I said, as if I actually believed him.

He pulled into the lot of my apartment, parked under a streetlight.

It was after midnight. I thought about Jamie. Sometimes he waited up. I imagined him on the sofa, in his jeans and shoes, wearing one of my old Air Force sweatshirts. His leg falling off the cushion, his head leaning crooked on the armrest. An empty carton of milk on the floor next to a box of cereal or something. The TV still on, blaring. Of course, he would be sleeping.

I might nudge him, saying, "Jamie." I might stay there with him, watching.

William had his hand around my neck. I knew what he was up to.

I slid down, moved my mouth over his boxers. He eased the seat back and as I heard him groan, I began to nibble. I took him, moving harder. My eyes watered. My mouth got sore. I kept on, hearing him tell me how much he really liked me. I felt his hand on my head tugging. He yelled for me, saying yes and yes and fuck me. I moved lower, into one thigh, then the other.

He kept calling me his baby, yelling harder, louder, grunting. I bit him, teasing, deeper. He kept asking for more.

I bit again, as if I were a tiger. I heard him scream. He yanked me.

I tasted something salty.

"Jesus fucking Christ," he said.

I sat back and put my hand on my mouth. It was dripping. I opened my door and spit on the concrete. I wiped my face with his jacket.

I took a closer look. "You're bleeding," I said.

There he was, with a wound like a gigantic peanut, the size and color of a plum. I told him it looked like a vagina. He said it wasn't funny.

He sat there with his legs spread.

His blood was bright. I said, "Maybe you're anemic."

I started thinking of the morning. I started thinking of my plans then. I pictured Jamie asleep. I tried not to look back. I thought about tomorrow.

I HAD TO CATCH

I knocked on the door eight times. A cow bellowed on the other side of the door. I pushed the little board up over the latch. It was an old barn, gray and wooden, one my grandparents had built, or probably the ones before them.

My breath pushed into the cold air. I had on a hat, mittens, and the boots I wore when I fed the calves every morning before I had to catch the school bus.

I knew what it meant when a cow was separate from the others.

I'd spent a lot of time up in the hayloft, tossing the bales that I helped my dad harvest—every summer, after picking stones from the dirt and throwing them onto a wagon to get tossed onto the stone pile that had existed since whenever—the fields would grow, and once it was time again, we'd go out with whatever the machine was called, and I'd catch the hay straight from the baler that would wrap the stuff with twine.

The baler would throw the things, shooting them like vomit.

I'd do my best to catch them, using my arms, and on the wagon, I would stack.

My hands were calloused.

I was tough. I was a girl.

RAYON

I hated the Army. My husband, Jimmy, and I joined so we could be together, but after our daughter, Whitney, came along, Jimmy got interested in everyone but me. By the time Whitney was five, he was with Terri, and Angel, then some chick named Bunny, or Baby. Jimmy and I kept things up for a few years, but things were never the same, so Jimmy got out of the army and went back to the States—he was in graduate school where he studied physical therapy.

I was left in Germany with six months to reenlist—I didn't know what to do. Then the Army got short on female MPs, and decided I had what it took. Some nights I worked as a cocktail waitress at the base nightclub, making extra money to pay for my divorce. I was working too much, but I never had to think about stuff like Jimmy, being alone, raising Whitney on my own.

My first two weeks as a cop they put me in training, but I still never had a clue. Week one I rode with a good-looking guy named Sanchez. He had dark hair and brown eyes kind of haunting, and he sucked Tic-Tacs and smacked on his lips. He had good lips, blackish-red and crescent shaped, all shiny and glowing. When he talked, I watched the lips.

Sanchez and I did stray dog calls, car alarms, suspicious noises. When we weren't driving we sat around in the dark, lounging in the coupe on the roadside, or off at Location Seven, the cops' hiding place—a little spot at the end of a long gravel road, tucked away behind a crappy brown shed.

It was a nasty place, but that didn't matter, 'cause I was feeling that way, like it didn't matter what I was doing or who I did it with. And I knew if I didn't get with the program, I wasn't going to have anybody to do *anything* with for a very long time. I knew Sanchez was interested, so I made sure he knew I was interested, too. We sat in the car and talked and smoked and I liked to watch him watch me move, so I did what I could.

He was from a place outside Chicago with cheap outlet malls and a big Six Flags' Great America. He followed the Packers and hated tattoos, and he kept a small tube of gel in his pocket to smooth down his hair. The stuff smelled like peppermint.

Sometimes other cops hung around that hideout, rolled down their windows, and lined the cars side-by-side. Then it was all cop bullshit and Sanchez forgot about me while he entertained his pals. One of the others who was there was this guy Jerry, who was my next-door neighbor. He was always hitting on me—Jerry was at the house, at the station, at the club. Jimmy had loathed him but I didn't think he was so bad. Sometimes he was funny. Not bad looking and he seemed to know how far to go with the jokes.

When Jimmy left, Jerry took over my lawn. It gave him an excuse to hang around my yard. He took good care of my grass, mowed it perfect, and let his go to shit. I liked to watch him while he worked, seeing him sweat—I offered him a beer when he looked like he was ready. Then we'd sit on my porch and he'd tell jokes, all dirty and crude. But I still laughed, cause they were all funny. I thought one night we'd end up having sex, and it gave me something to look forward to. I could tell he felt the same way, which made teasing about it, delaying it, even more fun. I didn't like his wife, Kay, because she was snobbish, like she was better than me, like I was some tramp next door, messing up her nice little bungalow. But I didn't care. Kay reminded me of the way I was with Jimmy— good and stupid, like that marriage thing was all perfect and rosy. That made me sick and I was tired of all that crap—it was time I had some fun. Besides, Jerry made me feel good and alive, like I belonged somewhere.

Week two I got a car to myself. I drove around, trying to act like I knew what was going on. I never did, but it was all new and fun and sexy in a way—a pistol hanging from my hip, out there in the night, smelling that air. It made me a little crazy in a strange kind of way. You can be doing nothing, but you have it all—the two-way radio, the gun and the car, and all of a sudden you're someone new. At first it's like a costume. But later on, you forget.

My first night alone Sanchez's voice cracked over the radio telling me to meet him at Seven. When I got there he was waiting, window down, sucking on his candy. I parked right by him so our windows met. I rolled mine down. Smelled his hair.

"What's up?" I said.

"Thought you'd be lonely out there on your own."

I looked at him, flirting, but not giving it all away.

He chuckled. "Got you something," he said, reaching toward his passenger seat. "Four leaf clover. Over by the range in the morning. First thing I thought of was you. Just my luck." He handed it over, dragging his fingers over mine.

"That's really sweet." I meant it even though I guess he was moving a little slow for me. Still, it *was* a sweet thing to do. Kind of kid-like. I messed with the clover in my palm, holding it gently.

Something came over the radio—Jerry taking care of something out on Day Street. Sanchez looked down at this radio, then back to me. "He's something, that Jerry."

"Yeah. He's all right."

"No, I mean *something*. Guy talks about you all the time."

"Yeah?" I blew on the clover a little, watching it move. "That's nice."

"You want to take it easy with him, you know? He's a talker. You don't want trouble, do you?"

I smiled at Sanchez. "Maybe I do," I said. "But don't worry about Jerry. I can handle him."

I got out of my car and leaned over through Sanchez's window. I gave him a little something I knew we both wanted. Then I backed off, smiling a little, tucking my bangs up under my beret.

Davies rolled up in his car and got out, standing between our cars. I got back in mine. Sanchez lit up and started puffing.

"What you guys up to?" Davies said. He leaned on Sanchez's coupe, facing me.

"Just getting by." Sanchez exhaled and some got in Davies's face.

Davies waved the smoke away, folded his arms over his chest. He had a great dentist: his teeth were the straightest, whitest I'd ever seen. His eyes were bright, boyish blue.

Sanchez and Davies talked Army. I listened, thinking how much I didn't like it. They both couldn't wait to re-up. Some people were just made for it, I guess. With Jimmy I was fine, but now I had to decide what I wanted and knew it wasn't sitting around talking cop bullshit on some army base in Germany.

"Hey. How's that girl, Sara?" Davies asked Sanchez.

I didn't have a clue. I said, "Yeah. How is she?"

He dropped me a look. "She's fine, Davies," he said. "I don't see her that much anymore." Sanchez looked at me and threw his cigarette out the window. It fell between stones and sat there glowing.

Sanchez got a call for a possible prowler, shook his head and started up. "You gonna be around?" he asked me.

"I have all night," I said.

I stayed there with Davies. He got in my car and started telling me how he wanted to be an artist, a painter. I listened, but was watching him the same way I watched Sanchez. He could tell too, cause after a few minutes he moved across the seat and started drawing with his fingers on my leg. I didn't try to stop him. I had always been faithful to Jimmy, but now I didn't have anybody to be faithful to. Just a little touch from Davies made me want him. I eased over, moving closer—we kissed hard at first, then softer. Then we left the car and went into the shed. It was all new to me, and I guess I let go something fierce—afterwards I felt like I'd been broken in all over again.

After Davies left I hung out by the shed, wrapped my arms around my knees, sitting on the hood of the cruiser. I felt free and open, like there was a new kind of harmony in the world. I was glowing. After a while, Sanchez came back and asked what I'd been doing. I told him not much, just taking in the sights. Then he asked if I would go to the movies with him the next night. I told him to pick me up at eight.

At home that night I put my daughter Whitney to bed and I dug out the anatomy book I'd used in nursing school—I was an assistant before the army made me an MP. I stashed Sanchez's four-leaf clover in the book figuring I might get it laminated. I knew it was stupid, but nobody but me would know. I could do what I wanted.

Sanchez was fifteen minutes early. He brought flowers, opened my doors, paid for everything. Just like Jimmy.

After the movie, it was sprinkling, so we ran for the car. He got wetter than I did, and when we got in the front seat, he leaned over, skimming my cheek with his lips. He did that all over my face for a while, and when he finally kissed me, the air got warm and sweet. The world seemed new and great, like I was on fire and in the middle of it all. He tasted like cigarettes and a little like orange. I wanted to take him all in, but I backed off. He said it was fine, we'd have time.

We had more nights like that, and after date three we made love at my place. Everything was fresh and new and worked like a charm—I could see us together for a while. He brought nice things for Whitney and me and was always in a laughing mood. We had things in common—working out, *ER*, hot cocoa in bed. Both Catholic, but didn't go to church. And the sex was perfect, though he always insisted we turn out the lights. After the second night he stayed over, I got the clover laminated and slid it into my billfold.

Jerry wasn't thrilled about Sanchez's blue Intrepid parked out in my driveway. I told him it was between Sanchez and me, but he said I needed to watch out for Sanchez, that he wasn't exactly what he seemed. I was flattered that Jerry cared enough to make that stuff up.

Last night was bikini night at the bar. I was out there working, hanging out in cut-offs and a blue rayon top. It was skimpy and thin, but I liked showing off once in awhile, prancing around with that fake smile. I made big tips cause I let the guys put the money exactly where they wanted. I needed the money, and it was good, too.

Since I was a new MP, other MPs came to the bar. When they asked for drinks, they ordered them strong. Usually they called me Sweet Linda, the bar girl, but sometimes I was their Pumpkin or Candy. New ones came up as each night went along. Like I was all theirs—even the next day, decked in cams in formation.

I was walking around with my top tied up in knots. Then came Jerry, Sanchez, Davies, and even a few others I didn't really know. When I saw them walking in, I went into the bathroom and looked in the mirror, making sure my make-up wasn't running and my hair was in place—I had it up in a high ponytail with a few red curls hanging over my brow. I straightened my top and turned to the side, pulling in my stomach a little, then smiling, trying to imagine how I would look in their eyes.

I knew why they came—they all drank at Jerry's before I started working here, so I tried to impress them and show off a little. I knew they'd like the bikini. I made sure it was perfect, and loosened the strap just a bit, giving them a hint of what was hiding underneath. When I had it the way I wanted, I walked back out to the bar and grabbed my tray.

They were sitting in my section and it was getting packed—lately business had been bad, so the place got a new manager, guy named Bob, who had things every night: dance marathons, costume events, raffles and rewards. Tonight it was bikini tops for the girls. Bob had new themes and getups coming: Daisy Duke Do

All, Cleavage Clamor, see-through nights, everything he could think of.

I shuffled through the crowd back to my section. Davies said hi and then looked right down at his old Doc Martens.

Jerry put up a hand so I could slap it. It was something he always did when he saw me. I reached up, touching his palm.

Sanchez nodded, smiled. He looked good, smooth. Just like always and better than the others, teasing me.

"Bikini night," I said, turning a circle so they could see it all. Everyone smiled and stared and I smiled right back.

Davies ordered Pepsi. Jerry ordered Blow Jobs and Bottom Bouncers, Slow Screws, anything with sex in the name. Sanchez drank Jack Daniel's. I gave them what they wanted—they gave me the tips.

Everything got crowded. I scurried here and there bumping, shoving all around. Loud music blared and boomed. People swung everywhere, except the MPs who just sat there all night drinking. Sanchez kept looking at me, smiling, telling me how sexy I looked, and I kept thinking about taking him in back. Jerry slapped his hand up again for me to touch it, and Davies got jittery from the caffeine in the Pepsi.

It was almost bar time and I went back to their table to bring the last round.

"Hey there, Kitten." Jerry slurred a little.

Sanchez put out his smoke, and while I leaned over to slap Jerry's hand someone pushed me from behind. I fell into Sanchez's lap, spilling the tray. Jack Daniel's and Irish Cream splashed in my face and on my top. It was sticky and I smelled like whiskey. Some guys fought from behind me. Bouncers waded in.

I tried to catch my feet, but things got awkward—people were everywhere swinging this way and that. I wiped my face so I could see and when I looked up, I saw Bob the manager staring right at me. I didn't want to lose my job, so I pulled myself up. I grinned at Sanchez and pulled up my bikini so it covered me again, then gave

Bob a little wave. I knew Bob liked me and sometimes he'd let me slide if I'd mess around with him a little after bar time.

At the end of my shift I slipped a T-shirt over my rayon top. When I walked outside, Jerry was waiting at my car. I was glad to see him, even though I knew he'd had more than he could handle.

"You OK there, Kitten?" he said, swaying a little.

"Sure," I said, getting out my keys, sliding past him to unlock the car's door. "You need a ride?"

"You gonna give me anything else?"

"Well, maybe," I said. "Doesn't look like you can do much tonight."

"I don't know bout that," he said.

"Just get in." I opened his door and eased him in. After I was in, Jerry was all hands—it didn't excite me, but it didn't bother me, either. We kissed and then I let him go up under my shirt. That seemed to satisfy him. After he calmed down a bit, I put the car in gear and drove him home—he was snoring by the time we got there.

That was last night. Tonight I was parked out at the flight line, staring at the rain on the glistening blue hood of the coupe. The radio scratched out a call for a domestic dispute—Andrews wanted it covered quick because the guy wasn't just army, he was military police. I clicked the wipers, the brights and the overheads, hit the siren and the gas as I reached for the two-way radio.

Jerry got there the same time as me. We slogged for the door, the uniforms soaking fast—that camouflage clung to our skin. I slipped over a Big Wheels and fell in a puddle, cracking my right shoulder hard, my 9mm sliding up on the sidewalk. I got it and was up, but Jerry was already laughing—I was slathered in mud. Lightning and thunder busted the sky wide open. But I was glad to be there, lights flicking around, rain pouring down, us with these guns. It was like a dream.

Jerry shoved me back as he opened the door, slipping his rounds in his Beretta. I did the same. My gun was stippled with grass and mud, so I was slapping it away when Davies came up from behind me.

"Who is it anyway?"

"Fuck if I know," Jerry said.

Jerry palmed the door handle and opened the screen a crack. There were shouts, something big busting, a kid screaming. Jerry yanked the screen and hit the paneling with his shoulder and we poured in, jumping this way and that, pointing the guns, everything jerky. My boots slid on the linoleum and I almost took out the fish tank.

My hands shook. Something big popped inside me like an electric current, like lightning smacking me—I remembered the time I called the cops on Jimmy. He did Angel at the bar—she worked there with me. When I asked him about it, he banged me up. I tried kicking him out, but he wouldn't leave until the cops made him.

This place was dark and tortured-looking, like a junkyard. Crap was hanging off the ceiling, and everything was torn up inside. The walls were gray like mud and there were holes everywhere. The kitchen was thirty days of filth, by the stench.

"Hey, man. It's him," Jerry said to Davies, talking quick but low and quiet. When I looked over, I saw a tall guy in shorts. Guy had hair like Sanchez, but there was a scorpion tattooed across his left shoulder.

The guy turned around like he had all day. I noticed the way he held his cigarette and moved his head, his eyes, that smile. About halfway through the turn I knew it *was* Sanchez.

I thought I might be sick. He was standing over this girl in the corner of the living room, toeing her with his boot, rubbing her, prodding her with it. He gave her a little kick in the thigh, and slid the boot up between her legs. It gave me the shivers and I kind of felt that boot. He was smoking, watching us, kicking at her gently, almost like he was taking a break.

"Jerry," he said. "What's happening?"

"Step away, Sanchez," Jerry said. He tipped his pistol down at Sanchez.

"And look who you got with you. It's *Kitten*! How you doing, Linda?"

"It's raining," I said. "You gonna let her up? Let her get some clothes." I was trying to be firm, but it probably sounded like I was pretending.

"Sara? She doesn't want to get up. She likes it down there, don't you?" He looked down at her while she crouched on the floor, covering her breasts with her hands. Sara was curvy and toned with ivory white skin, and the same tattoo in the same place as Sanchez. She was long and blonde and pale-faced with pouty bright lips.

Sanchez raised his cigarette hand. A kid was on the stairs screaming. I figured it was hers.

"Get the kid, for Christsakes. And get the girlfriend some clothes," Jerry said.

"Got it," I said, my voice still wavering. I holstered my gun and grabbed Sara's heap of clothes. I inhaled his second-hand smoke and dropped Sara's clothes in front of her. Blood dripped from her face. Sanchez watched her get dressed like it was a reverse strip show, taunting, grinning to himself, smoking.

I headed for the kid on the landing. He dug his head in the back of my legs, wrapping me up. He didn't care how wet I was, he just wanted a place to hide. He looked like he could belong to Sanchez. I grabbed the railing. It wobbled.

"So what you gonna do, Jerry, take me down?" Sanchez flexed his fists, showing muscle.

"C'mon, Sanchez. You gotta go down. You know the rules," Jerry said.

Sanchez walked over to the couch and put out the cigarette in a big pile of ash. It looked like he got a burn by the way he jumped.

Sara rocked in her corner. She looked like the loser in a monster game of paintball—blue stains on her skin, her blonde hair clumped with red blood in places.

For a minute there was silence. Then startling thunder and the kid screamed, sounding like a lawn mower as his cries dug into my pants. My nerves were wearing thin. I brushed my damp hair with my fingers, then squeezed the railing tight.

"Things between us are good, right?" Sanchez said, looking up at me. I looked back at him, squinting, trying to give him something mean. I knew my mascara was like war paint all over my face.

"I just need my smokes," Sanchez said.

Sara looked down. Sanchez slipped his hand under a cushion, feeling around. He grabbed his cigarettes.

Jerry and Davies holstered their guns.

The kid came out from behind my legs, jerking me a little. "Mommy," he said and everybody looked up at us on the landing. The rail wobbled some more and I almost fell over.

"I just want a smoke," Sanchez said. He sat down on the sofa, offered Jerry a cigarette, and they sat there smoking, puffing away like nothing ever happened. Davies was in an armchair that matched the couch. I could've choked waiting for those guys to finish their damn cigarettes, waiting to get out of that sick place and get some good air.

Sara got up and lay her head on Sanchez's shoulder, the clotted blood in her hair rubbing onto his skin.

Davies took Sara and the kid to the hospital. Jerry read Sanchez the card, then took him down to the station—Sanchez was up front, just like he was working. I followed. We had to fill out reports.

Jerry, Davies and I sat in a brown paneled room with dark tiled floors. There was a plain desk with hard metal chairs—they were government-issue, so everything was cheap. Davies sat behind me, rubbing my neck, my shoulders. "You OK, Linda?"

"Why wouldn't I be?"

"I don't know. Word is you just got out of, you know, something—"

"Like this?" I said. "Fuck you for knowing that. Fuck you for saying it to me." I got up off my chair, but I had nowhere to go. Maybe I was shaking. I turned around and shook my head at Davies, then ran my hand lightly across his dirty cheek.

Andrews sent me home to clean up. I put on a new uniform, redid my hair and makeup, tried to look good. Then I drove around trying to find something—work, fun, whatever. I thought about picking Whitney up from daycare.

My shift wasn't over.

I drove by the base nightclub, but there was no one there. After the storm let up, Davies met me at a cul-de-sac.

"That's some bad shit." He hung his elbow from the window, leaning out, reaching for my cigarette. I handed it over and checked the rear-view mirror. I focused on a tree's reflection.

"Whatever."

"Sanchez. He's just like that," he said.

"You could have told me sooner."

"Well, I didn't want to say much," he said, handing the smoke back. He stared at the ground for a minute. "That silk top you were wearing last night—"

"Rayon. It was rayon."

"It was nice. You looked, well, pretty." He moved his blue eyes onto me.

"Yeah," I said. I watched the cigarette burn, then flicked it with my finger. Ashes fell to the ground.

"Maybe we could start over. Like, dinner." He nodded his chin in the air, like he was pointing. He smiled, showing me his pretty teeth.

I sat there puffing on a smoke, watching him. I thought about that—did I want to? Sure, maybe, I didn't know. I couldn't decide right there on the spot. I wanted a man for all the things you need a man for, but I didn't know if I was ready or if Davies was the man. Maybe it didn't matter who the man was. Sanchez hadn't turned out all that well. Jerry was nice but he just wanted to play.

Davies looked good sitting in that car, that splintered light shining on his face. I thought about our night in the shed. It was good—he was no slouch. I smiled and thought he might be something to look forward to. He was still a kid, but decent. Maybe he'd grow up fast.

Streetlights glowed on new puddles, turning the water a funny shade of yellow. The moon was full like a soft face. The rain started again, so I watched it hash the puddles, listened to its rhythm, smelled its air. Seemed like everything was better in the rain.

I tossed the butt to the ground. "Just let me get through today, will you? You can ask again later if you want to. OK?"

I put my car in drive, held it with the brake a minute, then slid away from him.

OSHUN

The place is known for oysters. We've been here before, but today's our first time having oysters.

The waiter brings them on a plate. They all look the same with their hard shells, gooey in the middle.

We squeeze lemon over them, and I look at my friend with her long sleek hair covering her head like an umbrella.

We raise the shells to our mouths, sucking in the contents.

We laugh and talk about the Band-Aids of our pasts. The black cat she keeps losing. The strangers in my kitchen.

We toast, lifting our chins.

We raise our hands to get the waiter's attention so we can order something much simpler.

BABY

I'd been through more than some people, I guess—had trouble with my father until I was fifteen, then with guys in school, then a husband who shoved me around and when I got pregnant took up with my best friend. I got mad about that so he kicked me in the stomach and I lost the baby. Eventually I just quit and moved South, got a job as a kindergarten teacher. I loved teaching.

At a school function, I met this guy who was doing a story on kindergarten kids, a cute piece for the Sunday paper. He was tall and seemed decent, so when he asked for my number, I wrote it on a napkin. I told him I was Sara. He talked a lot, told me he was a widower. He had a sexy voice.

Monday night, he came over. Waiting for me he looked at my shelves, telling me which writers were his favorites. He told me his wife, Marcy, died two years before. She liked Kafka. We drove around, then went to his apartment so I could meet Baby, the dog who had been Marcy's seeing-eye dog after she lost her sight.

"You look just like Marcy," he said to me. This dog, Baby, was next to me, her chin on my leg, drooling. She was black and white with gray, a mix of everything.

"You look like all my ex-boyfriends combined," I said, grinning at William.

He handed me a beer and told me he'd only known her a couple months before her diagnosis, but that he took care of her and married her, even though he knew she would die.

"No kidding?" I said. I sipped, scanned his shelves, looking at the books about deafness, blindness, death. Stacks of William's unpublished novels sat on the bottom.

In a minute he was behind me, kissing my ear, whispering that Marcy had been raped twenty years ago and never got over it.

"That's one reason I stayed," he said.

"Hmm," I said, and took another sip.

We ended up in bed. He was a kisser and I hadn't been with a man since before I moved. William smelled like a cheap aftershave I liked. I figured maybe we should just enjoy ourselves. We went on but I got tired pretty quickly. I think he was just happy to have sex. When he walked me to my door I figured that was the last I'd see of him.

But he called the next morning and said he felt bad about pressing things and I told him sometimes things just happen. He asked me how I felt, and I told him I felt fine. He wanted to talk more so I said sure and he said he'd be over after work. I could hear the keyboards, the people talking in the background.

He was OK-looking and pleasant enough. I don't need a whole lot. He said maybe we could start over. I said, "Sure. That's fine."

He told me I deserved to live somewhere bigger and much nicer. He put his big hand on my leg, looked into my face. "I think I really like you."

"You like me in bed."

He told me I was smarter than any girl he ever dated.

I called my friend Angelina in Minnesota while I was making coffee, telling her I might have a date for her wedding.

"Not the guy you just had sex with," she said.

"I can teach him." I poured myself a cup of coffee. Some dripped onto the counter.

The next week, he stood naked while I waited on his sheets. "The radiation killed her," he said, hands on hips, staring up. "When I took her to the ER, she was already in a coma."

He looked like he was crying, but it was just the sweat on his face.

"I can live through anything," he said. "Someday I want children."

"Kids are hard," I said.

"We could have something special, something lasting."

"You don't have to say that," I said.

"You want to take a walk?"

He gave me a T-shirt and the orange shorts he wore to play basketball, and he told me about his dream to be in the NBA.

I talked about my guard days.

It was almost midnight. William led the way.

"This is the path I used to walk with Marcy," he said, "when she still could walk." He rested an arm on my shoulder.

"Seems like you really miss her," I said.

"I hope that doesn't bother you," he said.

"I can handle most things," I said.

"You want to take the leash?" he said.

I took the long red strap and called out Baby.

He said, "I've been with a lot of girls since Marcy."

"Jesus," I said.

"I want to be fair," he said.

I stood waiting by a pole while Baby stopped to pee.

He said, "I really like you, Sara."

I left and fed my kitten. William called right away and said, "I hope I didn't scare you. I thought that was why you left."

I lay on my mattress. My kitten bit my toes. I said, "You have certain things to deal with."

He said, "I think I love you."

He just kept on talking, saying that what he felt for me was something he hadn't felt since Marcy.

"I'm going to need a friend," he said. "Fall will be the hardest part."

"Have you considered therapy?" I said.

I called Angelina after hanging up with William, and I told her I was Marcy.

"Funny," she said. "How's that going?"

Kitten sat on my lap. Her eyes were big, the shade of William's.

The next night, William cooked. *The Godfather* played on the big screen. It was his favorite. I set my sandals next to William's.

He kissed me and told me I looked pretty.

He wiped his lips with a green napkin. Everything was green, I finally noticed. The carpet, the pillow, the dog's collar, probably Marcy's eyes. William told me my eyes were darker than his dog's.

He put his napkin down and looked at me and said, "If I knew you longer, I'd ask you to marry me. I'm scared you'll die."

"The doctor says I'm healthy."

Maybe he was trying. He took me to his room.

"Promise me one thing," he said.

"Yeah?" I said.

"Promise to be honest."

This seemed pretty weird, but it seemed to get him off.

He moved inside me harder.

"Say it," he said. "Say 'I promise to be honest.'"

He was dripping with sweat. The red glow of his face seemed to light the space around his head.

Angelina called as I was reading one of William's stories in the paper.

"You still dating him?" she said.

William stopped at my place. He was shining from his workout.

He said, "I really really love you."

He grabbed my breasts, but I told him to keep off them.

I went and took a shower. I wrapped the towel like a turban on my head and put on my robe. I went to the living room, where William was sitting on the futon, petting Kitten, who kept on biting him. His finger was bleeding, and he wiped it on his shorts. He looked like he was crying.

"You're still here?" I said.

"I want this to work. I don't want you to think that all I want to do is fuck you."

I laughed a little. "Yeah, OK," I said.

"Will you wait for me?"

"Wait for what?" I said.

"I'll go to therapy. I'll work on being honest." He looked at me, staring down the way he always did. "I'm not leaving you," he said.

"Go ahead," I said.

He put his big hand on my shoulder, and ran his bleeding thumb along my face. "I really like you, Sara."

I wished I liked him too.

I watched him walk away, and I shut the door behind him.

I HAVE MOTION LIGHTS

My neighbors sat, with paper plates on their laps. Some of them brought chairs of their own.

There really were no ground rules.

There were nuts in the house, a fruit assortment, sushi. Chips, salsa, hummus, veggies, dip. Beer and wine and ginger ale and Fresca. Someone carried over nachos and a cheese plate.

I'd spent the day cleaning, buying things at Target. Saying hellos to everyone around me.

Ever since my break-in, I took extra steps to spread myself with karma.

People ate. We laughed.

The back bulb went out.

My dogs sniffed. They lifted their legs and they peed on my zucchini.

BONES

Grandfather Sutton died of heart failure. Genetics, they said. I went to the wake, where I touched his cold hand.

Then my mother left my father. He was never around. Mother and I moved to a suburb, somewhere closer to St. Paul. Father went to California. He didn't come back, but never said why.

Mother and I went to Christmas dinner. Aunt Peggy fussed about backaches, groaning as she rose from Grandma Sutton's kitchen chair. She chuckled, saying if she didn't have so much weight to carry, she wouldn't have any complaints. Uncle Jim gave himself a shot of insulin. Cousin Cherie talked about her most recent gall bladder attack. So did Aunt Laura. Ran in the family, they said. We ate meatballs, and mashed potatoes. Stuffing, chicken, and tater-tot casserole. Then pecan and pumpkin pies. I had chicken, even though I was trying to be a vegetarian. Then everyone went for seconds.

Mother said her in-laws didn't like her because of her weight. After the divorce, she went from size 46 to 30. Then there was a stand-still. She tried Phen-Phen, Jenny Craig, the Protein Diet, saying nothing worked. She told me never to get fat. I was fourteen. And five feet, six inches, 131 pounds.

I was dating Sean. After six months, we talked about sex, but I wasn't ready. We came close a few times, but I always chickened out. Then he stopped calling. I would still see Sean at parties and when I went to the beach with my friends. He wore his tapioca-colored shorts, the ones he wore the first time he kissed me. I would dream of his brown baby eyes, that curly dark hair.

Mother worked for a mortgage company. After work, she hung out with her friends. Then she brought men home, but I couldn't remember their names.

Father's parents were stick-figure thin. Father was, too. But I didn't see those grandparents anymore. They said I should have kept my parents together.

I went to the beach with Gretchen and Amy. It smelled like fresh fish. We wore bikinis as we lay in the sun. The elastic of my striped suit pinched my skin. My friends told me I wasn't fat, but I never believed them. We talked about plans: who was having parties, the clothes we would buy, about boys and having sex. We splashed in the cold water, getting each other wet.

Mother tried the Cabbage Soup Diet. Her clothes got loose. Men noticed her. Ken, Jim, Ted, and Charles. Whomever.

Father called from California. He was planning a trip to Europe, he said, to buy expensive wine.

When I was little, Mother used to rock me in her chair. Headaches made me cry. Mother would comfort me as I rested my head on her large breast. She smelled like baby powder. She ran her big manicured hands through my brown curls, humming until I fell asleep.

I took the bus to the public library, where I read about calories, obesity, food, and weight loss: a BMI is a basic metabolic index: a person's weight in kilograms divided by height in meters squared. One inch is 2.54 centimeters, and one pound is 0.45359237 kilograms. Doing nothing in one hour, the average person will burn one calorie for every kilogram of weight (2.2 kilograms per pound).

A person's weight times 16 is the number of calories she needs per day.

My BMI was 21.1. The recommended BMI is from 18.5 to 24.9. Anything over 25 is overweight, and over 30 is obese.

I noticed fat people everywhere. Skinny people too.

Mother stopped cooking. She was on a new diet. (The Grapefruit one, I think.) She used to always be in the kitchen when she was with my father.

Mother bought new glasses: the small, round pointy kind. Then she dyed her hair blonde, bought expensive brand-name clothes, wore the trendy shades of make-up: kinds with names like Chardonnay and Moonlit Rose, the ones the newest models were wearing in the Revlon ads. She looked different every time I saw her, which wasn't very often. She and Michael laughed downstairs in her basement bedroom. Their noise echoed everywhere.

At first, the pounds dropped fast. In three weeks, I went from 131 to 120. I was within my recommended BMI, but I wanted that extra edge. My Guess jeans were baggy, but I still felt fat. With the money Father sent and the lunch money Mother seldom gave me, I took the bus to the mall, buying the latest styles: blouses, skirts and brand-name pants. I resisted my hunger. When school started again, my classmates told me I looked like Mr. Bones, the skeleton from biology class. Sean noticed me and told me I looked great.

Father used to call Mother fatso at the dinner table.

According to The Weight Control Information Network, from the National Institute of Health, "Obesity occurs when a person's caloric intake exceeds the amount of energy she burns. In one study of adults who were adopted as children, researchers found that the subjects' adult weights were closer to their biological parents' weights than their adoptive parents'. The environment provided by the adoptive family apparently had less influence on the development of obesity than the person's genetic makeup."

I was cold, but getting popular. People, even the stuck-up ones, said I looked great in my new clothes. I made the cheerleading squad, chanting for Sean, Spartans' wide receiver. I went to parties with Gretchen, Amy and my other cheerleading friends, where we drank Bud Light Ice that Amy's older sister bought. My friends slept at my house so we could stay out late. Mother was always out late, too.

Sometimes I didn't eat for days. Especially after going to parties with my friends. One can of Bud Light Ice has 96 calories.

Mother tried Dexatrim and Weight Watchers. Slim Fast. Saying she hadn't lost enough.

I hit 115. I did sit-ups in my room. In my dresser mirror, I examined my face, reminded that it was baby-like, not like the *Seventeen* models. My blue eyes were small compared to my round face and big lips. I was starting to look more like my mother. I applied make-up, trying new tricks to look good, putting pink blush high on my cheeks and rows of black eyeliner around my eyes, extending the line just a bit. I brushed my long brown curls, arranging them in different ways, examining each look. I pinched the skin of my cheeks, thinking that, no matter what, my face was still fat.

I started passing out. After Mother heard me fall down the stairs, she took me to Dr. Zunker, telling him she wanted a pregnancy test. I was still a virgin—I tested negative, but Mother insisted I go on the pill. I got the prescription to make her happy, even though I never took it.

One stick of a Kit-Kat has 120 calories, six grams of fat. A Quaker unsalted rice cake has 35 calories, zero grams of fat. One Chips Ahoy granola bar has 120 calories with four-and-a-half grams of fat. Thirty-five hundred calories equal one pound of fat.

My bones started showing. While lying flat on my back, I could balance a yardstick over my pelvic bones. I learned that in order to avoid passing out, I needed to get up slowly, and when you stand up too fast, the blood rushes to your head and makes you hit the floor.

I read the *Vegetarian Times: Beginner's Guide*, only reading meatless recipes, examining ingredients and calorie content. "Lentil and Golden Squash Pot Pie: 337 calories per serving, 15 grams of fat. Couscous Tabbouleh, 210 calories, five grams of fat." I fed myself through the words and pictures on the page.

Mother said, never get fat. Never overindulge. Never give in to your cravings. And when you do eat, take small, delicate bites.

Thanksgiving dinner. Laura and Cherie talked about getting their gall bladders removed. I pushed Aunt Peggy in her wheelchair. Jim pricked his finger for a glucose level. I smelled sweet potatoes and pies, and my stomach growled. I spread my food thin on my plate, and took small bites, rearranging the potatoes, mixing them with peas and corn to make it look like I'd eaten more than I really had. When Grandma Sutton asked me why I didn't want any turkey, I told her I was a vegetarian. On the way home, Mother said she never knew. She complained about having eaten too much, but said at least she hadn't gained back the weight that she'd lost.

At a keg party, at someone's house whose parents were out of town, I celebrated my fifteenth birthday. Sean talked to me, telling me I was looking really good these days, that he wanted me back. We left the party, and went to the nearest parking lot, where we made out in his car—he blasted the heat, making the windows get steamy. His breath was like fire. As he kissed my ear, he suggested we do it, so we crawled in the back seat, where he slid on a condom, and then slid off my jeans, moving in me like quicksand. I lay in the back, staring at that church steeple while he tore me up inside. When I told him it hurt, he moved even faster, making me bleed. When he was done he held me tight, then told me he loved me. His arms made me warm. When he drove me home, he smiled, wishing me a happy birthday, saying he'd call. I told Gretchen and Amy, who were flirting with the possibility of being non-virgins.

Father called from Europe, telling me how great it was.

Mother stopped asking about sex. She told me I looked good, thin. I wore extra clothes to keep myself warm. My stomach growled. I ate as little as I could get away with, doing sit-ups in my room. Jumping jacks too. I examined my reflection in the mirror, pinching my cheeks.

I was the bridesmaid for a distant cousin's wedding. I zipped the bride's white gown while she held in her stomach. At church, I walked down the aisle with a boy named Pete. After the ceremony, I leaned on him, and he asked me for a kiss. I told him I was taken. Then everyone ate chicken, while I peeled the frosting from my cake. At the reception, I caught the bouquet.

I slept in. Mother didn't know—she left for work early. I walked to school, missing my first class, Home Economics. I didn't want to learn about sewing, gardening, or any of that stuff anyway. The kind of stuff Mother used to do. When I finally woke up, I went to the school office where the fat secretary gave me late slips and detentions. I served them during lunch hours where I rested my head on the desk and woke up when the bell rang.

I stepped on the scale—100. I waited for Sean to call.

I completely avoided foods with fat. According to Joyce Vedral's *The Fat Burning Workout*, "If your diet consists of 40 percent fat, as does the average American, you are fat-even if you are not overweight. And chances are you feel fat, too, and not just to the touch. You feel sluggish—not as energetic as you would feel if your body were comprised of a higher percentage of muscle."

Mother laughed with Fred, Charles, Tim, and Phil. I didn't know all their names, but I didn't care. Their colognes lingered, invading the kitchen where the refrigerator took up space.

I was 95, and light, almost free: light-headed meant light-hearted. Sean talked to me at another party, apologizing for the last time. He loved me this way, he said. I followed his lead—I felt safe and warm in his arms. He touched me, saying he'd call.

Calories burned per 20 minutes: Stair machine, 260. Running, 220. Cross-country skiing, 220. Swimming, 210. Rope-jumping, 200. Aerobic dance, 200. Race-walking, 160. Bicycle-riding, 140. Walking, 110.

I was hungry, but ignored the rumbling in my stomach, reminding myself how good it felt when my jeans were loose around my waist. I shivered, remembering to hang on to something when I got up.

A three-fourth cup of Garden Rotini has 210 calories, one gram of fat. A two-third cup of Penne Rigate has 210 calories, one gram of fat. Three ounces of Firm Tofu has 50 calories, two-and-a-half grams of fat. One slice Country Hearth whole wheat bread equals 100 calories, and one-and-a-half grams of fat.

Christmastime: I went to holiday parties and my relatives watched me eat. Grandma Sutton waddled, struggling to carry her extra weight. She told me to put something in that tummy. Mother didn't say anything, just that she'd overeaten. With each spoonful, I felt inches of fat growing on my thighs.

I saw Mr. Bones in biology class, wondering if I really looked like him, what it would be like to be him.

I cheered, now for basketball games. Gretchen and Amy too. I was on the top of the mound. I did cartwheels, calculating the calories I burned as I kicked my legs. Sean was a Spartans forward—he dribbled the ball, then took a shot, scoring with his big hands. I yelled, "Way to go, Sean!" Mom worked, then went out with her friends. Father sent money, but forgot to call.

Naked, I stood in front of the mirror, squeezing the skin on my thighs and feeling the fat beneath it.

I visited my grandfather's gravesite, asking him how it felt. If heaven was really as good as they say.

I opened the refrigerator door. It was cold and empty inside.

Sean talked to me at a party, saying he wanted to get back together. I thought I might be delirious from the Bud Light Ice. Sean was out of condoms, but we still had sex. I subtracted the calories as I thrust my hips. He said I love you, pulling out. Then said he'd call, but didn't. I built up my courage, calling him—his mother said he wasn't around.

I hit 89. I told no one as I ignored my pangs of hunger.

According to Ken Sprague's *The Gold's Gym Book of Weight Training*, "There's no getting around the fact that vanity is endemic to our collective American personality—why else would you care so much about how you look? Yes, you could rationalize paying attention to your appearance as a social necessity."

I heard Mother downstairs with Frank or Ken or whatever. She came upstairs in a lacy black bra and pink flowered panties, her skin hanging. She smiled. She seemed happy.

At Easter Sunday dinner, people ate. I said I didn't feel well.

One-fourth cup of Uncle Ben's Long Grain Rice has 150 calories, zero grams of fat. One-fourth cup of Florida Gold Orange Juice has 110 calories, zero grams of fat.

I saw Sean in the hallways at school. He said hi, but kept on walking.

Mother got a call from vice-principal Jep. He told her I'd been late nearly every day since the New Year. I had 22 detentions. The next step was suspension. Mother took me to Dr. Zunker, not asking if I was pregnant. He told me to gain weight. I lied and said I would.

Practicing for the upcoming season, I cheered, burning calories. My blue skirt was loose, my pom-poms were heavy, but I liked that weak feeling—it reminded me of my power. Gretchen and Amy asked if I was OK. Using my cheerleading voice, I told them everything was fine.

People stared. I was cold and my cheeks were hollow. I went to my cousin's baptismal feast, where I avoided the ham and turkey and Grandma Sutton tried to make me eat apple pie. I ate a bite to prove a point. Peggy talked about her back surgery. Uncle Jim talked about his recent diabetic diagnosis. I went home and did sit-ups, jumped rope, and looked in the mirror. I ate nothing for the next three days.

Mr. Jep called Mother a second time. I was suspended for being late again. Mother took me back to Dr. Zunker, who referred me to a diet therapist named Judy who was fat and told me to eat five small meals a day. Then I saw a blue-eyed, gray-haired therapist named Dorothy who told me to tell her about myself. As I talked, she put an open palm over her chest, asking me how I felt.

Never, ever get fat.

Sean stopped talking to me at parties, didn't even want sex—he told Gretchen he was afraid he'd break my bones. I told Gretchen he didn't matter anymore, even though he did.

Mother took me out for meals. First to Yuki's, then China King, the next week it was Planet Hollywood, the Rain Forest, or who even knew. She watched me eat. When I looked up, she smiled.

I felt guilty for every bite I took, weighing myself every two hours even though Dorothy told me not to. With every inch of flesh that returned came the achy feeling that my world would cave in.

Mother said she was sorry. I looked at her sad face. She took off her glasses.

Father called, saying life was great.

The scale said 95. I wondered if Father was right.

I went to a family reunion where people sat at picnic tables. Kids ran in circles, playing tag. I fed my cousin milk from a bottle. Back pain, gall bladder attacks, heart failure, diabetes. High blood pressure. People ate potato salad, coleslaw and ham sandwiches. Dessert.

Grandmother Sutton had a stroke. Said soon she'd be meeting her husband.

Mother laughed downstairs with Ted, Mack, Sam. Father forgot to call. Sean ignored me. Fat Judy told me what to eat. I talked to Dorothy and cried.

Never get fat. You need to gain weight.

I read more books about food and health and fitness. Vegetarianism.

I went to the beach with Gretchen and Amy. We wore bikinis and compared tan lines, resting on towels, soaking in sun. I looked at their thin bodies and high cheekbones, noticing how pretty they were. Thinking, how happy they must feel! We rubbed tanning oil, making ourselves shine. I told them they looked good. They said I did too. I forged a smile, massaging the lotion onto my body, thinking of how nice they were, trying to make me feel so good. Sean walked by, so I got up, and without looking back, I ran for the water, splashing, and then diving, getting wet and cold, the water stinging my eyes and forming beads that stuck to my skin. I came up for air, gasping for breath and went underwater again, trying to stay under as long as I could.

I went to Grandmother's funeral. Genetics, they said. The family lulled around, heads hanging low. I looked at my grandmother's face. Mother touched Grandmother's hand, then she reached for mine.

We sat on a hard pew. We stared ahead in silence, taking in the air.

ONE BELOW

Amy and Gretchen and I rode around in Gretchen's parents' Explorer, sliding over slick spots on the road, trying to find things to do. We'd already been to SuperAmerica, waiting for other classmates to show up to spread the word about a party. But there was nothing, so we had a few beers in the lot until we saw a cop car driving by. Then it started snowing.

I was still fifteen, but Amy and Gretchen were sixteen, and Gretchen had a fake ID, and sometimes went to bars. The drinking age was nineteen, and we looked it with our heavy make-up. Tonight we had our hair teased up with hairspray. Gretchen put dark liner on her eyes and spiked up her short dark hair. Amy's hair looked blonder, and she wore pumps to make her look taller. I tried my best to have a special look, wearing loads of pastel on my eyelids. I dyed my hair really blonde last summer with peroxide, which dried up all the ends. Now I wore it in a big banana clip.

Gretchen drove to the lot of Boomers as a last resort. She shuffled through the lanes, trying to find a spot. "Looks packed," she said.

"I bet there's lots of guys," Amy said, looking in the mirror. She reapplied her lipstick.

I sat in back, and popped my head between the two front seats. "You think they'll let us in? Don't they check IDs?"

"Remember, I dated Taylor, Mr. big head bouncer?" Gretchen said. "I'll vouch for you guys."

"Maybe we shouldn't," I said.

"Eileen, you wouldn't believe the guys," Gretchen said, pulling into a spot, then turning off the car.

"Should I bring my coat?"

"Like, yeah. Unless you want to freeze," Amy said.

We stepped out of the Explorer and shuffled across the lot. Gretchen slipped, then caught herself. Snowflakes fell, caking up our hairspray. I could hear the music booming from inside. We stopped around the corner by the entrance, getting in a huddle. Two guys passed us, staring, then moving on. Everyone had frosty breaths, red cheeks and our lips were getting chapped. It was one below.

We sat at the bar, drinking screwdrivers. It was packed, people moving all around.

"I feel funny," I said.

"Be confident," Gretchen said.

"If you look shy, it'll give you away," Amy said, sipping on her straw.

Gretchen said, "I told Taylor I'd give him a little something, so you guys really owe me big time."

"Let's do shots," I said. "I need to get relaxed."

We did Absolut. People were up and bumping at the bar. The bartenders couldn't keep up. Smoke was everywhere. We were getting drunk.

"Let's dance," Amy said.

"I'll stay here and save our seats," I said. "I feel a little queasy."

Amy and Gretchen danced with all the other people banging hips and elbows, getting hot and sweaty. Amy flung her body all around and Gretchen twisted her waist, rotating her hips, clapping her hands up.

While taking nervous sips, I looked at the rows of liquor bottles behind the counter, the bartenders shuffling from the fountains to the fridge, filling cups with ice, uncapping beers and mixing drinks, ringing up the register. Customers left big tips on the counter.

Amy and Gretchen were crowded in the middle of the floor, dirty dancing with two men old enough to be their fathers. Amy's hair flung everywhere, getting in her partner's face. Gretchen's shirt jumped up when she raised her arms, and her skirt hiked up. Her partner crouched lower, bending his knees and swaying his butt, his eyes even with her belly button. Some bit hit was playing.

I thought about getting up to dance. It was a big collage of people, shuffling around, yelling and singing, flailing everywhere. I stayed in my spot. I had to watch the coats and purses.

A tall guy with big dimples and dark lips stepped up, holding his money over the counter. I admired his chestnut-colored hair. He looked in my direction, and I looked at someone's cigarette that was burning in an ashtray, pretending not to see him. He patted my right shoulder.

"Anyone sitting here?" he said, pointing to Amy's chair.

"Um, no, go ahead."

"You alone?" he said. He sat.

"My friends are out there dancing." I pointed to them.

He finally got the big-haired bartender's attention and ordered a martini. He left a tip and ate the olive. "Well," he said. "I'm here alone. You want a drink?"

I wondered if he was old enough to be there. I'd had enough so I said no. He got me a Budweiser, telling me I had to at least hold on to something. He said his name was Lee and that he lived in California, where he went to college. Now he was home for Christmas break, visiting his family. He asked me what school I used to go to.

"I'm not really from here. My friends and I went to high school in Chicago."

Lee nodded, sipped on his martini. "Not nineteen, yet, huh?" He smiled.

I looked at the moisture dripping down my bottle's neck.

"It's OK. I used to do it too when I was younger," he said.

I looked at his dimples, then studied the rest of his features: his squinty eyes, his little nose, his clear thin face. "OK," I said. "I go to East. I'm almost sixteen. My name's Eileen."

"Pretty name," he said, unwrapping his scarf. "My sister is Eileen."

A bearded guy with curly hair almost fell on me. He spilled his drink on my skirt, then apologized.

I said it was OK, and wondered where my friends were. I saw them on the highest speaker, dancing like they sometimes did at home with the stereo turned up. I laughed a little, knowing they were having fun. "Those are my two best friends," I told Lee, pointing to them.

He turned back to look. "They're having a good time."

"It's our first time here. Gretchen used to date the bouncer."

"You must feel awful in that skirt. I can get you something dry. Looks like they're having fun without you."

I looked at Lee. He seemed nice enough. "I'll have to tell them. I have their coats and purses."

I got off the chair, almost falling over. I shuffled through the crowd, stepping to the platform, hopping up, standing behind my friends while they danced around like strippers.

"Hey!" Amy said. She spun around.

"Here's your stuff." I set their belongings on the floor behind them, then looked down at all the people, feeling on stage. "I'm leaving," I said. "I found a boy."

Amy screamed. Gretchen asked what was wrong, dancing in a circle.

"She found a guy," Amy said.

I looked down in his direction. "The guy leaning by the bathroom in the leather jacket."

Lee took me to his home in Indian Trails, a wealthy subdivision where my mother had driven my sister Jill and me the week before to look at Christmas lights. I remembered my mother admiring his display.

His BMW crunched over his long drive. "My parents are in Austria, but my sister's home, so we have to tiptoe."

His room was in the basement. It was huge and glorious. Everything looked crisp and clean and neatly placed. A big screen

TV was angled in the corner and a stereo lined one wall. The floor looked almost marble and the walls looked like a finely finished silk. His bed was centered in the middle, as if on display. I thought I was in heaven. The only thing that was a off was that I felt a little tipsy. Things were spinning just a bit.

Lee gave me a pair of navy sweatpants and a California T-shirt. I went to the bathroom and changed, smelling the freshness from his softener.

Lee said he'd find us some good music.

I sat on the bed and told him thank you for the sweatpants. He picked something by U2, then sat next to me. We talked for a little while about school and college, and then he leaned over, kissing me. He undid my banana clip and tossed it on the floor. We made out, then lay on the bed.

I had goose bumps so he turned up the heat. I looked at the ceiling, thinking everything was spinning, so I sat up and he sat next to me.

"You're not a virgin are you?" he said.

I felt a little awkward, sitting there without my shirt and bra. "Well, no. No, I'm not a virgin."

"Good," Lee said. "I wouldn't want to, well, you know, do anything to hurt you."

I looked at the smile on his face, at his big cute dimples, and I smiled back. We made out a little more and took off the rest of our clothes. He had a big penis. He told me I was little. He touched my breasts, then touched between my legs as I tried looking at his eyes. He lay on top of me and I touched his back. He tried to push himself inside me. I stopped kissing, hoping to get his attention, but he was too into it to notice, so I tried to slide away. He finally was still. "Is something wrong?" he said.

I said, "I don't think I'm ready for that yet."

"Oh. OK," he said.

I thought that was pretty easy and was glad that I said something. Then we kissed, and after making out a little more, he tried again. I got tense and nervous, so he backed away. "I thought you might have changed your mind," he said.

"I don't know," I said. Things were back to spinning, so I closed my eyes. Again he moved his penis up against me, pushing in the space between my legs, and I was tired of saying no and I wanted him to like me, so I closed my eyes tighter—I suspected it might hurt, like it had the first time. But this time things didn't work. Lee was too wide and since I wasn't wet, he wouldn't fit.

We lay there, listening to drumming from the radio, then the words: Sunday bloody Sunday. It was my favorite song. He asked me for a blowjob. I hesitated. I said I didn't know how.

"Just don't use your teeth," he said.

I moved down and sucked his penis, and he tugged on my hair, moving my head the way he wanted. It didn't take long for him to come and when he did, he held my head against him, forcing me to swallow.

I gagged, so he let me go. I spit up on his stomach.

"You did good for a first time," he said, then got up and fetched me a towel from the bathroom. I wiped my mouth and asked for something to drink. He put the towel in the hamper and got me a glass of water.

"This stays between us," he said.

"Oh?"

"I'm twenty-three," he said.

"Oh?" I said, taking a sip.

"I'm an adult," he said, taking the glass from me. "You, you're technically a child."

I woke up hung over.

"I hope you don't get in trouble for being out all night," Lee said, getting his keys.

"My mom won't know," I said.

We rode in silence, and I felt like throwing up, so I tried to avoid looking out the window. When we got to my street, I gave him directions, and as he pulled into the driveway, he laughed a little bit.

"Something wrong?" I said.

"Well," he said, "my parents own this place."

I told him goodbye and wished him well in college, hesitating, debating whether to offer my phone number, or to wait until he asked, but he didn't, and as I stepped out of the car and watched him drive away, I thought maybe he forgot.

My sister Jill was sitting at the table, and my mom was making coffee in the kitchen. "Who was that boy in the nice car?" my mother said.

"His parents are our landlords."

"How'd you meet a boy like him?"

I started for the bathroom, and yelled to my mother down the hallway. "A stupid party at our school," I said, then shut the door and leaned into the toilet.

I took a nap and later woke to the ringing phone. It was Amy. We decided to go to Kroll's Restaurant to discuss the night before. Gretchen picked us up, but we didn't talk until we got there.

"How was your guy?" Gretchen said.

"Fine," I said, thinking I was better off keeping some things to myself.

Gretchen and Amy talked about the men they'd met on the dance floor. The men bought them drinks at bar time and walked them to the car.

When the waitress came, we ordered coffee. Amy and Gretchen compared their men and talked about kissing.

They seemed so happy.

I told them I was happy.

I was happy. I was happy. I was happy.

DARLING

In the car, my son Mark leans into the floor. He screams. He sounds like a man.

I want to ask if he's been taking drugs, but this question might upset him.

"You'll be OK," I say.

I speed through a red then swerve to avoid a big truck on my left.

Mark says, "Someone's out to kill me. I'm confused. My neck hurts."

At the ER, I start to write down info: names and numbers, checking boxes that ask about his history.

I know hospitals and particularly this one, since I used to work here. Now I live in another state. When I'm back here I stay at my boyfriend Leo's, a guy I met two months before moving. I was in this town for grad school and left for a job as a professor, where I teach literature and writing. Leo's a music professor here, currently on break, visiting his family in Cyprus. I came back this time to tend to his house, his pianos and his garden.

After I give the attendant back the clipboard, I sit. I take my son's hand. It's sweaty. His face looks pale. He says to me, "Please help me."

A woman in blue scrubs says, "His temperature is up there." She takes us to a curtained room in back. She shows us the bed and helps me help him get there.

After she leaves, I cover Mark and touch his head. He shivers. I say, "Darling."

He says, "I'm throwing up." He looks a little pasty. He says, "I need a pan."

I bring him a trashcan. He vomits and vomits and vomits.

He wears a gown.

I touch his forehead. It's hot. He's full of sweat. "Honey," I say.

He says to me, "Please help me."

A nurse comes, saying "He needs an IV." He gives her his arm. It's limp. I stroke his head. Like his days as a little boy, a toddler. Ear infections and pneumonia. Once he broke a knuckle.

She wipes his skin, then inserts the needle. He doesn't flinch.

Fluid drips into him.

We wait for labs. I'm versed on the other end of all the testing: specimens coming through the tube shoot, entering the system. CBCs and PTTs, UAs and at times a crossmatch. I worked that career for years, training in the army, where I met the man who used to be my husband.

Mark wakes. His eyes are glossy, wet. He says to me. "Where are we?"

I say, "You'll be OK."

"They're killing me," he says. "I'm confused. Please help."

I get up and squeeze his hand. "Shh." I hum to him, like when he was a baby.

He looks at me like he did the time I found him maybe drinking. "Huh?" he says, drowsing back to sleep again.

The doc says, "The tests are normal, save an elevated white count. Negative for mono. Negative for strep. Drug panel shows nothing. We have to do a lumbar."

I know from my days that may mean meningitis. I'm not sure what to say.

Though my son is sleeping, the nurse comes in to inject more meds into his IV. She says, "This will calm him. A lumbar can be painful."

Then the doc returns with his big needle and tray, two nurses, and two men in black security outfits with badges. I've seen lumbar punctures. I assisted in collecting marrow—stood with the tray waiting for samples. I remember most the moaning: one patient on his side, spine exposed. His feet were calloused.

I wake my son and say, "Darling." I help him reposition. I say, "Let's get you on your side. The doctor needs a sample."

He looks stiff. The two security men lean on him, then one says, "We need to keep him steady."

I also lean. I face him. Touching his cheek, like when he was a baby. "Hold my hand," I say. "Squeeze it hard. Break all my little knuckles."

Mark looks drunk. His skin feels hot, his eyes glossy. The needle is long and thick. As it starts into his back, the doctor says, "Picture a chemical equation."

As Mark tries to steel himself, I hum a tune I used to play on the piano, humming louder as I sense the needle disappearing into him.

The men lean on him. One says, "What's your thought on baseball?"

The doctor says, "Almost there," positioning his arms, keeping his legs planted.

Mark cries. He says to me, "Please help me."

From a floor high up in the hospital I look out at the sign that says, "Welcome to Champaign." I watch as people walk to their cars in the lot.

Mark sleeps. He smells like melted cheese. Signs on the wall say, "Precaution. Isolation."

He has meningitis, and we're waiting for results, hoping it's viral, which increases his chances of survival. My heart feels like it has burst and its parts are pumping through me.

I think of whom to call. I only lived here for a year. Leo's gone. I've been staying at his house, and Mark has been staying with his friend Rob who lives in a duplex with his mother.

A masked nurse comes in with his stethoscope and cuff. He nudges Mark, saying, "Mark," his voice muffled. Mark groans. I decide to call his father, who works as a pathologist in Maine. I stand by as Mark dozes off again, sweating, his eyes sealed and crusty. His hair is slick and shiny. There's blood on his lip.

The nurses wear gloves and gowns and slippers. The doctor smells like dusty sweat. It's two a.m. The doctor says, "The tests are inconclusive."

He says, "The labs tell me it looks viral, but nothing is definite."

I say, "Are you sure?" I've seen spinal fluid under many scopes, and you either see red and white cells or you don't. The white means bacterial. If viral, only red ones.

I say, "I've never heard that."

The doctor rearranges his Cubs hat and says, "We'll give him meds to cover the whole spectrum."

Mark twists and turns, and the doctor says, "He's lucky."

I think to call my mother. I still have to call Mark's friend Rob's mother.

I say, "I used to work the lab here. We moved a lot. I teach English in Michigan."

The doctor says, "Oh?"

I point to his hat and say, "You from Chicago?"

He says, "I like the Cubs."

"Mark, too. I prefer the Tigers."

The doctor scribbles and says, "We can quit the isolation."

"Can I have a copy of the labs? My ex-husband's a pathologist. He's coming in the morning."

After the doctor leaves, I read the IV bags and write the contents on a note pad.

Later that night, I decide to call Leo. His mother answers, saying, "Yassou," which I know, I think, in Greek, means hello. Leo taught me some things.

I say, "Can I talk to Leo?"

The mom says, "Leo, Leo."

"Leo there?" I say.

In Greek, I only know "hello," and some other words Leo taught me in the bedroom.

His mom says more things in Greek I don't understand.

I just keep saying, "Leo," and then she hangs up.

I watch Mark sleeping. His eye twitches. I pull the sheet over his bare toe.

I turn on the radio, then scan through the stations and get nothing but fuzz. Mark kicks off the sheet, so I cover his feet again, which look bigger than I remember.

Looking out, I see groups like insects. The sun blares, so I close the curtains. I hear moaning. "What is it?" I say and Mark says, "I think I see a jarhead."

I touch his hair.

"Don't leave me, Mom," he says, and then he's asleep again.

My cellphone rings. It's a number I don't know. I let it ring another time before answering.

"Hello," I say.

"Hello."

I know from the voice, it's Leo.

He says, "The sea does wonders for my hands, for inflamation. How's the house?"

I think I hear laughing, a woman.

I say, "I'm with Mark."

Mark screams.

"I'll call you back," I say.

Leo says, "Are you OK?"

I say, "We'll be just fine now."

The doctor is clean. His cologne is overdose. He wears orange pants and a blue crisp shirt, and while he talks about the lymphs and neutrophils, I try to remember how they look under the scope: the lymphs are smooth and purple, the neutrophils are splotchy, grains. The doc says we'll probably never know if it's bacterial or viral.

Mark sits, sipping.

The doc says, "The brain can get infected." He scratches his ear.

Then comes my ex-husband. I last saw him years ago in Portland for a conference. Now he looks bigger, old with muscles, his skin dark, his eyes small and slanted. His hairline recedes.

"Hey," he says.

I say, "You missed the doctor."

He says, "You're right about the cornfields."

"Huh?" I say.

He says, "This town is a cornfield.

He stands by Mark's bed. "Hey, Son," he says.

Mark waves.

"You don't look so bad," Mark's father says, "except you need a haircut."

Mark laughs. He says, "Ouch it hurts to laugh," and then we all laugh.

After Mark falls asleep again, my ex gets out his computer and shows me new pictures of his baby.

"Nice," I say, thinking the baby looks a lot like our son. I look at Mark. "He's sleeping a lot," I say.

My ex-husband says, "You look terrible. You should probably rest some."

At Leo's, I lay on his bed, wondering who's here with him when I'm not. My suspicions were right with my ex-husband. I'd left him when Mark was just a baby.

I smell the sheets. They smell like Leo. The phone rings.

"Hello?" I say.

The high-pitched woman on the other end says, "Would you like to buy some vacuums?"

After hanging up, I study the stuff on Leo's desk: his newest CD of nocturnes he composed and then recorded: a picture of his tuxedoed self leaning on one of his pianos—the day before the pic, he got his hair dyed—that whole month he did extra sit-ups at the gym, rode the bike every day for an extra twenty minutes. A few times, we met each other in Chicago, walking down Michigan to our usual places like Armani, where I sat on a bench and watched him come out of the fitting room with his potential pants, a jacket or a blazer. It was where he bought his suit. Once I tried on a dress, though I knew I couldn't afford it.

I put the CD in, then lay on the floor, remembering the songs as he composed them. I'd be upstairs with my laptop, staring at the hardwood. Once I found a long blonde strand of hair on his pillow. I'd watched him with a woman performing in his concerts, them bowing and collecting their applause, returning for an encore.

I read the CD case, like the one I have at home. The dedication on the insert is to me: "To Eliza Straus. I will always love you."

I listen as the music slows then grows quiet and then loud again. Staccato and crescendo.

I step out on the deck. After seeing the high grass, I go out to the shed and wheel out the mower, but then as I pull the handle, nothing happens. So I remove the oil cap and turn the mower over. I watch the oil drain, then add the stuff I bought the week before from Fleet Farm. This try, the mower starts nicely. I push it through the rough spots. Getting close to the house, I accidentally cut the lavender, which he'd said his ex-wife planted when she used to live there.

As I mow, I wonder about the potential of his garden. I like his house. I like his deck, and inside, I like to play on his pianos. I like his nice bed, and his TV is humongous. I love to bathe in his

Jacuzzi. Pink and red stripes line the guest room walls. Mark doesn't like to stay here.

In the front, I mow into a rosebush. "Oops," I say. The vibration of the mower sends me surges.

I look up and see the neighbor, waving, juggling his groceries. When I wave back the mower cuts out and I figure I'm close to done anyway, and I probably did a better job than Leo would have, since he's always scared of ruining his fingers.

"Hey," I say to the neighbor, who once told me he traveled the world in his band, although he can't read music. "My music is shit," he'd said. "Leo's world class. I'm nothing in comparison."

I put the mower away and go inside and make myself a sandwich. I look in Leo's cupboards. I find six jars of olive oil in tall shapely bottles. I look through his mail, sorting through the bills I'm supposed to pay with his checkbook. A dime falls from my pocket. From his stack, a picture drops: of him, and a girl possibly my son's age. Leo smiles in the picture. His students are young. This one's blonde hair covers half her face. She wears shorts. The back of the photo says something Greek-looking.

Leo's phone keeps ringing. I keep answering and it's always something different, this time a solicitation for a boys' camp. The voices are alike. A woman. That same high pitch.

I finally take a shower and go back to the hospital, where my ex and the doctor talk, nodding heads. They handshake.

Mark is on his side, facing me. "I'm hungry, Mom." he says. He's only been allowed soup and juice and water.

"Rob came," he says, "with his mom. They brought me pop."

"You saw Rob?" I say.

Mark moans. His hair sticks to his scalp and he still has that sick smell. His arm feels hot. I get a wet cloth and put it on his forehead.

His dad says, "We're pretty lucky." He holds Mark's hand and I have the other. After a while Mark says, "that's enough," taking his hands back.

After Mark falls asleep again, his dad says, "How's the boyfriend?"

I say, "He really isn't."

"That's too bad," he says. "I was hoping you were happy."

I say to him, "I am."

He turns on the TV. The screen shows a hound pawing at a turtle. He says, "I'm sorry I wasn't a good husband."

"You already said that."

Mark screams.

I say, "He thought someone was after him. I thought he was on drugs. I didn't think of meningitis."

My ex's phone rings and he puts up his finger and goes out to the hallway.

A lady tiptoes in to give me a number she says I need to call in order to take care of my bill and talk about insurance. My ex has gone to his hotel room.

Mark sits. He says, "Remember when you used to read me Shakespeare?"

I say, "Shall I compare thee?"

I say, "To a winter's day?"

"It's summer, Mom," he says. He rolls his eyes.

"My little genius," I say.

When he was a toddler, he'd bring me book after book after book, asking me to read to him. Didn't matter what the book was—he'd plunk it on my lap. He'd climb up, resting his head on my chest. I'd rock and as I read the words, I'd watch his eyes get wide. After about a dozen pages, he'd fight to keep them open. He did that until his early teens. Now when we're at home, he reads alone in his room, though he never leaves the door shut.

I worry about the bill. I've worked hard to make a better life for us: leaving his father, then the army, then going back to school. Though I still worked part-time as a med tech, I was so poor that we relied on food stamps.

Mark says to me, "I'm starving."

In the cafeteria line, I see a tall gray-haired man I used to work with. I remember once in the lab, him telling me he never found women attractive. He looks at me and gives me a smile that I realize is ingenuous.

"Jim?" I say.

His green scrubs hang like curtains. "I used to work with you," I say, and then I think maybe it isn't him.

Back in the room, Mark eats his bagel. I'm on hold again, waiting to talk to someone about insurance.

"This bagel rocks," says Mark.

I say to him, "Be gentle," and finally someone comes on the phone: a deep-voiced man who says, "You only have a co-pay."

As Mark showers, the Zest smell becomes so overpowering, it makes the room start to even look a little cleaner.

He puts back on his street clothes. He says, "I'm missing buttons."

I say, "Maybe I can fix them."

When my ex comes back, he opens his computer to a shot of Mark holding a wrench up like a trophy. "Last summer he helped me build the deck." Mark seems so short in the picture.

My ex says, "Next summer, I'm taking him to see my grandma in Jamaica."

We were married for three years. I never met his family. I've never been to Jamaica. I say, "I think he'd really like that."

In my ex's rental SUV, the three of us pick up Mark's friend Rob and drive to the closest place to eat, which turns out to be one where we can eat peanuts from a bucket and throw the shells on the floor.

My ex asks Rob, "What's up with the earring?" and as Rob looks down, breaking open a peanut, my phone rings in my pocket. Then comes the waitress in her skirt and lipstick.

I say, "I'll have a baked potato," and my ex says, "I'll do ribs." Mark and Rob order chicken soup.

Mark gets up and says, "I have to use the bathroom," and as I watch my ex follow him, I realize they move alike. They look like brothers.

When they come back, Mark sits by me, saying, "I can't eat."

He rests his head on my lap.

My ex takes Rob home, then Mark and me back to the hospital so I can pick up my car.

In the lot, my ex says, "It was great to see you."

He taps my son's head and waves to me.

He says to Mark, "I'm so glad you're OK, Son."

I step out and let them say goodbye to each other. My ex has a flight to catch. He has to get back to his family.

At Leo's, Mark says, "Can I play piano?" He sits at the one worth more than Leo's house, the one Leo uses for perfecting and has tuned as often as he has his hair cut.

Mark's been playing music since before I left his dad. I'd sing and rock with him while his father was out for the night.

He has his father's knuckles. They look like rocks.

He plays beautifully. He's never taken lessons.

After a while he gets tired, and falls asleep on the sofa.

I get greens from the fridge and make a salad, thinking I'll sleep eventually. I start looking through a closet, finding an umbrella and an oboe I haven't seen. After a while, I realize I haven't heard the phone ring.

I try to reach my mother, but she's not answering.

In Leo's mailbox, I find an envelope to me from Leo, post-marked from somewhere in Greece. Inside is a paper heart, a note saying, "Honey, how I love you."

I go up and run the water in his Jacuzzi, putting on the Schumann we always listen to while in there—we take separate ends, facing one another, our limbs like branches.

In his walk-in, as I thumb his vests, I think I hear his phone ring. I walk toward his phone and it stops.

Pictures of cows and horses hang in Leo's guest room. I look at myself in the full-length. On my face, freckles make collages. Mark stayed here only once before, but said he didn't like it. He said he didn't know why.

There were times when I worked night shifts. I carried beepers, going home on call. Before Mark was old enough to stay alone, if I was called in, I'd have to take him with me. Middle of the night, driving in a snowstorm. Fog clouded us in England. In Germany, I only biked, so I'd ride with him in back. We almost got hit once. It didn't matter where we were. People needed things. At times they even died there.

Back in Michigan, Mark and I live in campus housing. The floor is cold and tile, the walls cinder. The rooms are small. It's our little home. It can be pretty cozy.

Here I sit at Leo's biggest grand with my fingers on the keys, placing my thumb on a middle C like Mark did as a toddler. He'd sit on my lap on the hand-me-down piano we were gifted when in Europe by an airman who defected.

I stumble over the keys, remember playing at a recital once when I was a freshman.

I read Leo's music. I remember him performing, the crescendos and staccatos. Watching the size of his hands as they soared over the octaves. I try to play the music of my son.

I pack our bags. There seems so much to put inside them.

My son is seventeen.

His eyes are closed. He has thick long lashes. His hair is dark and curly, and his lips are the same curved shape as when he was a baby. He lies on his back, his body so tall, his shoulders broad, with muscles. Over him the sun shines, making his skin glow.

I get close. He smells like sweat.

From somewhere, I hear a clock tick.

For a long time, I just stay.

I watch the rhythm of his chest, seeing him breathe.